Trina nodded, but he wondered if she'd taken in what he said. "I suppose I should go to bed."

But her tone wasn't firm, and she stayed sitting on the edge of his bed.

"That would be a good idea." But he didn't move, either. He couldn't tear his gaze from hers, stupid as it was to keep staring at her. He'd used up his reserves of willpower in that last retreat. What he needed was a cold shower, although he knew any effect it had would be temporary. Finally, he heard himself say her name. "Trina." Nothing more.

She rose to her feet as if he'd tugged at an invisible string. Took a step. Then another. His heart pounded so hard, he heard it. The blood it was pumping was heading south, not to his head.

She whispered, "This isn't..."

"A good idea." He knew that, but no longer cared, not with her in touching distance.

HIDE THE CHILD

USA TODAY Bestselling Author

JANICE KAY JOHNSON

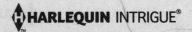

For Jeff Hill, consummate woodsman,
reader and generous friend.

ISBN-13: 978-1-335-52674-8

Hide the Child

Copyright © 2018 by Janice Kay Johnson

Recycling programs
for this product may
not exist in your area.

This edition published by arrangement with Harlequin Books S.A.

For questions and comments about the quality of this book, please contact us at CustomerService@Harlequin.com.

Printed in U.S.A.

An author of more than ninety books for children and adults (more than seventy-five for Harlequin), **Janice Kay Johnson** writes about love and family, and pens books of gripping romantic suspense. A *USA TODAY* bestselling author and an eight-time finalist for the Romance Writers of America RITA® Award, she won a RITA® Award in 2008. A former librarian, Janice raised two daughters in a small town north of Seattle, Washington.

Books by Janice Kay Johnson

Harlequin Intrigue

Hide the Child

Harlequin Superromance

A Hometown Boy
Anything for Her
Where It May Lead
From This Day On
One Frosty Night
More Than Neighbors
Because of a Girl
A Mother's Claim
Plain Refuge
Her Amish Protectors
The Hero's Redemption
Back Against the Wall

Brothers, Strangers

The Closer He Gets
The Baby He Wanted

The Mysteries of Angel Butte

Bringing Maddie Home
Everywhere She Goes
All a Man Is
Cop by Her Side
This Good Man

Visit the Author Profile page at Harlequin.com.

CAST OF CHARACTERS

Gabriel Decker—His US Army Ranger unit is the only family he's ever known. Recuperating from a possible career-ending injury on the ranch he co-owns, he takes on the task of protecting a teammate's sister...and the little girl who threatens a killer.

Trina Marr—A psychologist who works with traumatized children, she takes on Chloe's safety as well as her emotional recovery from the tragedy she witnessed. Trina never expected to have to defy the police, run for her life or put her complete trust in a stranger, a man who understands loyalty but not love.

Chloe Keif—Three-year-old Chloe is the only witness to the murders of her parents and brother. Trauma leaves her mute...but can she name the killer if she regains her voice?

Boyd Chaney—Retired army ranger, now, along with Gabriel Decker, owner of an eastern Oregon ranch. Still a ranger at heart, he's ready and willing to provide backup.

Michael Keif—The brains behind Open Range Electronics and half owner. Was he murdered for control of his company? Or did he uncover a dark secret?

Ron Pearson—"Uncle Ronald" to the Keif children, Pearson is co-owner of Open Range Electronics. He doesn't seem to have anything to gain by the death of his friend and partner. Or does he?

Philip Risvold—Lead detective investigating the horrific murder of businessman Michael Keif and his wife and young son. With the investigation stalling, he wants control of the sole witness to push her to speak...or does he have something else in mind?

Daniel Deperro—A dedicated police detective, he is uneasy about a leak from his police department that endangered a woman and child. When he finds the answer, he might have to make a life-changing decision.

Prologue

Squeezed into the tiniest space, Chloe tried not to look through the narrow crack where the cupboard door hadn't completely closed, but sometimes she couldn't help herself. Daddy was lying there right in front of her. All she had to do was crawl out and— No, no! Mommy said she had to stay here and not make a sound. Not even a teensy sound. Mommy said to wait, no matter what she heard or saw.

But she could see Daddy's face, and the face of the man who bent over him, too. Except… No! Mommy *said*.

Hugging her knees to squeeze herself into the smallest ball possible, Chloe closed her eyes. Tears wet her cheeks and she could taste them. She shuddered, trying to hold back a sob.

"Shh. Stay right there," Mommy had whispered. "Don't move a finger or make a sound. No matter what. Do you understand?"

She didn't understand at all, but she was scared, and she was *almost* doing what Mommy said, even when tears dripped off her chin onto her bare arms. Chloe peeked. Daddy's eyes were open, but she could tell he didn't see her. Or anything.

Now she couldn't see anybody else, but she heard the man talking. There weren't any other voices, but she didn't move. She didn't whimper, even when the house became quiet and stayed quiet for a long time. She had to wait until Mommy came or Daddy woke up.

She didn't move, didn't make a sound, even when different people came. They all had the same color of blue pants. Now she saw a man crouching beside Daddy, and even though she didn't move, she didn't, he lifted his head and saw her.

Her teeth chattered and she shook all over, but he stepped right over Daddy and opened the cupboard door all the way. He bent low, his face nice, and held out a hand.

"You're safe now, honey. I promise."

As he reached for her, the sob burst out, but not another sound.

Mommy said.

Chapter One

"Shall we leave the frosting white?" Trina Marr had already mixed up a cream cheese icing to go on the cupcakes cooling on a rack. "I might have some sprinkles. Or let's see." Being obsessive-compulsive neat, she knew right where she kept the small bottles of food coloring. "Green? Red? Or if we use just a tiny bit, pink?"

The little girl looking up at her nodded vigorously. The pigtails she'd started the day with sagged crookedly.

"Pink?"

Another nod.

Trina had become accustomed to the lack of verbal response. As Dr. Katrina Marr, she specialized in working with traumatized children. Three-year-old Chloe Keif had started as a patient but was now her foster daughter. Chloe still wouldn't talk, but she relaxed with Trina as she didn't with anyone else. She'd remained stiff and unresponsive in the receiving home where she was first placed. An aunt and grandparents both were hesitant to take Chloe when she had such problems. Offering to foster had seemed a natural step for Trina, if a first for her.

"Ooh," she said now. "You know what we could put on top?"

Chloe waited, bright-eyed and expectant.

Trina rose onto tiptoes to reach a jar in a high cupboard. "Maraschino cherries. Have you ever had one?"

A suspicious shake of the head.

"They're super sweet, like candy. The flavor just bursts in your mouth when you bite into one." Trina wrinkled her nose. "Don't tell anybody, but every once in a while when I'm feeling mad or sad, I open a jar and eat every single cherry." She winked. "Which makes me sick to my stomach, but I don't care."

Chloe laughed, then clapped her hand over her mouth, eyes wide with astonishment and…fear? Yes.

It was the first sound to come out of her mouth in the two weeks Trina had known her. She crouched and tickled Chloe's tummy. "It's okay, cupcake."

That almost earned her another smile.

"It was really smart of you to stay quiet when the bad men were in your house, but you're safe now. Anytime you're ready, you can start talking. You can make all kinds of noises." She blew a noisy raspberry. Neighed, like a horse. Revved, like a motorcycle engine.

And Chloe giggled again.

Heart feeling as light as a helium balloon, Trina

swung Chloe up to sit on the kitchen counter. "Here, try your first maraschino cherry." She opened the jar, stuck a fork in and popped one into her own mouth. "Yum." She offered the next one to the little girl, who sniffed it cautiously, then touched the tip of her tongue to the cherry.

Chloe's face worked as she savored the taste before she opened her mouth and snatched the cherry off the fork.

Trina waited for the verdict.

"Yum!"

Trina grinned and said, "Then let's make our frosting pink." Her mouth fell open. "Wait. You talked."

Chloe's freckled nose crinkled mischievously.

Laughing exultantly, Trina swung her to the stool she'd pulled up to the counter. "Now you're just teasing me."

The little girl nodded. It was all Trina could do to concentrate on how many drops of red food coloring she ought to add to the bowl of icing to turn it a pretty pink.

Her delight was quickly dampened by the sobering knowledge that once Chloe really began to talk the police would be ready to pounce.

If investigators had a clue who'd murdered her mother, father and older brother in their home, they hadn't confided as much in Trina or even hinted when pressed by reporters. Admittedly, the crime was not only horrific, it was puzzling. Chloe's mother hadn't been raped. Expensive electronics weren't stolen. Neither was the nearly thousand dollars in Michael Keif's wallet that had been left on the counter of the island in the kitchen. His Piaget watch, which according to the detective sold for over ten thousand dollars, remained on his wrist. If Michael, a wealthy businessman, had been the target, why had the rest of his family been killed, too?

Chloe wouldn't have been mute and terrified when she was found if she hadn't seen her father murdered within feet of her hiding place. With the investigation seemingly going cold, the detectives had latched on to the hope that this preschool girl could crack the case. It was making them nuts that so far, Chloe hadn't been able to answer a single question.

Trina worried about what the weight of their expectations might do to Chloe. What if she was never able to tell them anything, and had to live with that failure for the rest of her life?

But there was another really scary possibility. Somehow reporters had learned that the three-year-old survivor of the massacre couldn't say a word. On the local TV news, they'd even flashed a photo of Chloe as the anchor talked solemnly about the mystery and the devastating impact witnessing the horror had had on a little girl. Chloe had said her first word today, and Trina didn't want anyone else to know. Because…what if this incredibly vulnerable child became a threat a killer couldn't ignore?

Trina shivered. *Pay attention*, she told herself. She had to be careful not to turn this frosting bloodred.

GABRIEL DECKER SWUNG his rope with practiced ease. The loop settled on the ground just in front of a calf's hind legs, tricky to do in such tight quarters in the temporary corral. The second the calf stepped into the loop, Gabe pulled in the slack, wrapped the rope around the saddle horn and drew the calf toward the fire. Once a pair of wrestlers tossed the struggling calf to his side and pulled off the rope, Gabe would coil it up and go back for another one. Today, four ropers and four teams on the ground were moving things along well. They aimed by the end of the week to have every spring calf branded, dehorned, castrated and vaccinated.

His eyes stung from the dust cloud raised by bawling calves penned in the corral and their mothers milling outside it. Unpleasantly reminded of a dust storm in Afghanistan, Gabe had to keep pushing the memory back. The work demanded focus. At least he felt useful, which he hadn't much lately. He was irked that he couldn't be one of the men tossing the calf and holding it down, a task he'd performed by the time he went to live on a Texas ranch when he was fourteen. Size and muscle were appreciated for that job, since even two-to-three-month-old calves could weigh up to two hundred pounds.

Now he was lucky to be able to sit astride for hours at a time, although he'd suffer for it later. Actually, he was already suffering but refused to let anyone else suspect. He'd been wounded before but never taken so long to heal.

This had been a bad one, though. An IED had thrown him into the air and he'd landed poorly, breaking his femur on top of the damage done to his pelvis by the explosion. The doctor had suggested age might be an issue. A twenty-two-year old healed faster than a man closing in on forty, he'd said with a shrug. Gabe knew that, at thirty-six, he was close to aging out of active duty with his Army Ranger unit. But damn it, he wasn't ready to hang it up yet!

He'd tightened his legs in a signal to his gelding and gripped the rope in a gloved hand to start swinging it, when his partner waved him over to the side of the temporary corral.

Boyd Chaney rested one booted foot on a lower bar and his forearms on the top one. "If you're hurting, take a break."

Gabe stared expressionlessly at his friend. "What makes you think I hurt?"

"I know you," Boyd said with a shrug.

He did. They'd served together for a decade and become best friends. On recent deployments, Gabe had missed Boyd, who had been shot and crushed beneath his jeep when it rolled two years ago. He'd spent the next year in rehab and conditioning, trying to achieve the state of fitness required for their elite ranger unit, but had finally accepted that he'd never pass the physical. Unwilling to accept a desk or teaching job, he'd retired to the Oregon cattle and cutting horse ranch the two men had bought together with an eye to the future.

"I can manage," Gabe said now, tersely, and reined his horse back into the melee. Even over the bellowing cattle, he heard Chaney call after him.

"Stubborn bastard."

Yeah, so? Since that was the working definition of a man tough enough to make it as a spec-ops soldier, Gabe didn't bother responding. He'd make it back. He told himself that every day. Two, three more months, tops. But right now he could contribute here on the ranch. A little pain had never stopped him before, and it wouldn't now.

"I'LL BE THERE in ten minutes," Detective Risvold said.

"No!" Trina was in her office, seizing the chance to make the call between patients. In the past week, Chloe had made enough progress that Trina felt obligated to report that there was hope she'd soon be able to talk about what she'd seen.

Trina was thankful she'd been careful not to tell either of the investigators who called her on a regular basis where she "stashed" Chloe during working hours. That had been Detective Deperro's word. When he used it, Trina had almost said, *Oh, when I'm not home, I keep her in the third drawer to the right of the sink* but had managed to refrain. If either of the men possessed a sense of humor, she had yet to see it.

"What do you mean, *no*?" Risvold snapped. "She's talking, and you know how much is riding on what she can tell us."

"I wanted you to know she's begun speaking." Already regretting she'd made this call, Trina leaned on the word *begun*. "She's not back to natural chattering, and if I even tiptoe toward asking about that morning, she goes silent again for hours. Anyway, how is a three-year-old's description going to clinch anything for you? If I asked her to draw her father, it would be a stick figure. You do know that, don't you? What little she can tell you would be useless." She paused. "Unless you have a suspect?"

The answer was slow coming. "We're looking at a possibility," he said grudgingly. "Several 911 calls had come in from that neighborhood in the week before the attack on the Keifs. Someone may have been casing houses."

"But you told me nothing was taken."

"The guy may not have had robbery on his mind. He might have been a nutcase looking for the right opportunity."

Making it a random crime. It happened, of course, but rarely. So rarely she had trouble buying it now. "Do you even have a good description of him?"

"One of the homes he wandered around had security cameras. We have footage. If we have confirmation from the girl about what he looks like…"

Her eyes narrowed. The girl? What was with these guys? Were they deliberately trying not to see Chloe as a real person? Maybe cops had to do that, because keeping an emotional distance was healthy for them, but she didn't like it. "So you'd arrest him if she says the man had brown hair and brown eyes, and that matches the camera footage. Even though half the men in Sadler meet that description."

More silence. There were undoubtedly things he wasn't telling her, but...

"From what I understand, you didn't recover any weapons or meaningful trace evidence."

"No weapons, but we have a wealth of fingerprints and hairs we can match to the killer once we have him."

Usually he said "or killers." Had he become enamored of the idea of the wandering nutjob? And unless, say, they'd found a hair in the blood, she wasn't convinced. The Keifs probably entertained. Chloe's six-year-old brother had undoubtedly had friends in and out, the friends' parents there to pick them up and drop them off. Maybe in the kitchen to have a cup of coffee. However tidy the house, there were bound to be hairs or fingerprints or whatever that didn't belong to family members.

But investigating was up to the two detectives. Her obligation was to protect Chloe.

"I'm sorry," she said firmly. "She's not ready. I wanted you aware that she has begun to speak, that's all. When I'm sure she can handle it, I'll let you know."

They sparred some more, with her the winner—although she wasn't so sure she would have been if either investigator knew how to lay his hands on Chloe while Trina was tied up with her patients.

TRINA AWAKENED WITH a start. Her phone must be ringing, she thought blearily as she reached out to grope for it on the bedside table. If that annoying Detective Risvold was calling again—

Except…did she smell smoke? With returning consciousness, she realized the shrill scream wasn't the phone. A fire alarm downstairs had been set off, and suddenly the one in the hall up here began to squeal, too.

Trina shot up to a sitting position, fear punching her in the belly. Her eyes watered, and when she inhaled again, she bent forward coughing. There was a sharp undertone to the smell that she knew she ought to recognize.

Chloe!

Trina grabbed her phone and dropped to the floor. She crawled faster than she'd known she could to the door and into the hall. Even in the dark, she could tell the smoke was thicker here, and she heard the roar of fire. Heat radiated from the staircase, and when she turned her head, she saw flame burning up the wall.

No escape that way.

She crawled into Chloe's room and kicked the door shut behind her. *Block the crack at the bottom.* She'd read that advice before. A door could slow the flames.

Nothing she could use lay in easy reach. Like Trina, Chloe seemed to be obsessively tidy by nature, which meant no dirty clothes strewed the floor. Trina gave it up temporarily and pushed herself up. Heart beating wildly, she hit the light switch, but nothing happened. Then she ran to the bed and shook the small figure that formed a lump beneath the covers.

"Chloe! Wake up!"

A snuffling sound was her only answer—and if anything Chloe drew herself into a tighter ball.

Trina yanked back the bedcovers. "The house is on fire." Somehow she kept her voice calm. "We have to get out."

The three-year-old sat up. "I don't know *how* to get out," she whispered, and then jerked. "Look!"

Trina turned to see the orange glow already beneath the door. How could the fire move so fast? She yanked the comforter off Chloe's bed and hurried to cram it against the base of the door. Then she said, "We have to go out the window."

Nothing to it, she thought semihysterically. She unlocked and lifted the sash window, peering down at lawn that in early April was still winter brown and probably rock hard. She could scream for help... but what if men who had set the fire came instead of neighbors?

Gasoline, that's what she smelled. This fire hadn't started with a spark in the wiring or a frayed electrical cord.

After shoving the window screen until it popped out and fell, she said, "Come here, sweetie."

Chloe obeyed, thank goodness. Trina rushed to the bed for the two pillows and, leaning out the window, dropped them to the ground. They looked puny below. What were the odds they'd help break a fall?

But she couldn't think what else to do. Remembering her phone, she picked it up and dropped it, too. It bounced off one of the pillows onto the dark ground.

A sheet. She snatched it from the bed, horrified to see that the door glowed fiery orange and was dissolving before her eyes.

Twisting the sheet into an impromptu rope, she tied one end around Chloe's waist. Then she cupped the child's face with her hands. "I'm going to dangle you as far as I can with the sheet, but then I'll have to drop you. Just let yourself roll, okay?"

"No!" Chloe flung her arms around one of Trina's legs and held on frantically. "I don't wanna! Please! Don't make me!"

Throat tight, chest hurting, Trina said, "We don't have any choice." She wrenched a squirming, fighting Chloe away. Maneuvering her out the window was a nightmare, with the sobbing child flailing and trying to grab hold of her again. Finally, she was able to start lowering her.

The sheet ran out sooner than she'd hoped. Heat seared her back. She was out of time. *I have to drop her.*

But somebody ran across her yard and positioned himself below the window. "Let her go. I've got her."

Trina recognized the voice of a brawny young guy who still lived with his parents on the block. With a whimper, she released the sheet and saw him catch Chloe.

The fire behind her had become so intense she

didn't hesitate. She climbed out, turned and grasped the edge of the window frame…and let go.

ACHING, STILL FILTHY, grateful for the pain meds that kept her from fully feeling the burns and bruises, Trina sat holding an armful of little girl. Her position was awkward, rocked to one side so that most of her weight was almost on her hip. Her back and butt had been slathered with ointment and covered with gauze before nurses helped her put on scrubs to replace her ruined T-shirt and flannel pajama bottoms.

"There's some blistering," the doctor had told her. "Minimal, but you had a close call."

No kidding.

"It's going to hurt," he'd continued, "but if you have someone who can reapply the ointment, and if you take the pain medication as prescribed instead of trying to tough it out, I won't insist you be admitted."

He hadn't asked if she had anywhere to go to, given that her house had just burned to the ground, but she'd called one of the two partners in her counseling practice. Josh Doughten and his wife, Vicky, had become good friends. Good enough to be a logical choice for her to call in the middle of the night. Plus, their two daughters were both away at college, so Trina knew they had empty bedrooms. Josh hadn't even hesitated; he said he would get dressed and come immediately for her and Chloe.

But they wouldn't be able to stay with the Doughtens long. She couldn't endanger Josh and Vicky.

What Trina wanted to do was jump—okay, climb slowly and carefully—into her car and drive away. Far away.

Two problems with that. Her car had been in the attached garage and was presumably part of the "total loss" the fire captain had described. Problem two? So was everything in the house, from her clothes to her purse, wallet and credit cards. The only thing she'd salvaged was her cell phone. Until she visited the Department of Motor Vehicles and the bank, she couldn't even pay for a motel. Assuming anyone would rent a room to a crazy-looking woman with bare feet, wearing scrubs and carrying a kid who didn't look any better than she did.

The police would probably offer her and Chloe protection, but it would come at a price. After all her effort to hold them off, they'd have the access to Chloe they'd been so desperate to get. In phone messages left in the last day and a half, initial begging had progressed to pestering and finally threatening. They didn't understand the damage they could do to a fragile young child by trying to dig out answers too soon. And yes, Trina sympathized, but the murder victims were dead. Arresting the killers wouldn't bring Chloe's family back. But she was alive, and protecting and healing her had become Trina's mission.

As if she'd conjured them, the two men entered the cubicle where she waited. Risvold was middle-aged and softening around the middle, his blond hair graying. His partner, in contrast, had to be over six feet and was strongly built. His skin was bronzed, whether from sun or genetics, and he had black hair and dark eyes.

His eyes as well as Risvold's latched on to Chloe with an intensity that made Trina want to shrink back. Her arms tightened protectively.

"I already talked to the arson investigator," she said. "I'm sure he'll give you his report."

Detective Risvold slid one of the plastic chairs to face hers, and sat down with a sigh. Deperro hung back. Good cop, bad cop?

"I'm sure he will, but his job has a different focus than ours," Risvold said. "So I'd like you to tell us what you saw and heard."

"Just a minute." She stood up with Chloe in her arms and left the cubicle. Several people glanced up from where they sat at the nurses' station. "Excuse me. The police are here to talk to me. Is there any chance someone could hold Chloe for a few minutes so she doesn't have to be there?"

A motherly looking nurse leaped up and volunteered.

"You won't take your eyes off her for a second?"

"Promise."

Fortunately, the little girl was still asleep, a deadweight when Trina transferred her to the other woman's arms.

Then she returned to the cubicle, where she repeated her story briefly.

"You hadn't seen anyone hanging around?" Risvold asked. "No car parked on your block that didn't look familiar? Think hard, Ms. Marr."

She was really tempted to remind him that she was actually Dr. Marr. Not something she usually insisted on, but this man's condescension raised her hackles. "The answer is no. I didn't see anything out of the ordinary."

"The faster we're able to hear what, er, Chloe saw, the sooner you'll both be safe."

Hurting, scared and mad, Trina said, "If I were you, I wouldn't make her your focus right now. For one thing, it's obvious your wandering crazy is off the table as a suspect."

"What do you mean?" Gee, Detective Deperro spoke.

"I mean, would he have it together enough to understand that a small child might be able to identify him? And know where she was staying? Oh, and set the fire without a soul seeing him?"

Deperro's jaw tightened.

She leaned toward them. "Try looking at your own department, why don't you? It's been nearly a month since the murders. Chloe and I have been fine. The day before yesterday, I told you she'd begun to speak, that I thought it wouldn't be long before we could try asking her questions. Then tonight someone set my house on fire when the two of us were asleep inside. How many people knew what I told you? Who did *they* talk to?"

"Miss Marr... Katrina." To his credit, Detective

Deperro looked worried. "What about her day care? Is there anyone there who would have talked?"

"No," she said flatly. "And since even you don't know where she is, how would the killer have known who to cozy up to for news about Chloe?"

"I'm authorized to give you twenty-four-hour protection," Risvold offered.

Even without a plan, Trina said, "Thank you, but no."

He frowned. "But where will you go?"

Long-term? The correct answer was *I have no idea*. But she only shook her head.

Chapter Two

Not two minutes after the cops had left her alone, Trina knew what she to do.

Call her brother. Three years older than her, Joseph had never let her down, any more than she would him if he ever needed her. He'd be mad if she didn't turn to him.

Unfortunately, he'd take at least a day to reach her, but she and Chloe could surely stay with the Doughtens that long. Trina went out to check on Chloe, but the nurse smiled and rocked gently. "If you need to do anything else, she's fine," she whispered.

"Then I'll make a call," she said gratefully, and returned to her cubicle.

Her brother's phone rang once, twice, three times. It wouldn't be the middle of the night for him, or even the crack of dawn. Georgia was three hours ahead, which made it…eight o'clock there.

"Trina?" he said sharply.

She started to cry. She hadn't yet but couldn't seem to help herself now. Lifting the hem of the faded blue scrub top to wipe damp cheeks, she said, "Joseph? My house burned down."

"What? How?"

"It was—" She had to breathe deeply to be able to finish. "Arson. It was arson."

He swore. "Do the cops think it's random? There's no reason you'd be a target, is there?"

She took a deep breath. "It's a long story."

"Tell me," Joseph demanded.

The story didn't take all that long, after all. He had already known that she was now a foster mom, although she hadn't explained the background. Now she did.

At the end, she said tentatively, "I don't know what to do. I was hoping..." She hesitated.

"I'd come?"

The tension she heard told her the answer would be no.

"You know I want to be on the next flight to the West Coast. But I don't see how I can. We're wheels up tonight, Trina."

He was the one who'd shortened her name, to their parents' frustration. They'd been determined she would be Katrina, but ultimately even they had started dropping the first syllable.

She could call them...but she couldn't put them in danger, either. Joseph... Joseph was different. He could handle any threat.

"I'll wire you some money," her brother said.

"Thanks, but... I have money. I just have to get some ID so I can claim it."

"Okay." He was silent long enough that she was about to open her mouth when he said in a distracted way, "I'm thinking. I can ask for an emergency leave."

"You'd have said that in the first place if it was so easy."

"Yeah, it's not. We've been training and studying intel on this op for the last month. The major won't be happy."

He wasn't supposed to have told her as much as he had. Her heart sank, but she knew what she had to say. "Then...then I'll think of something else. I could hire a bodyguard." From Bodyguards 'R Us? Feeling semihysterical, she wondered whether that was a subject heading in the Yellow Pages. Craigslist? The bulletin board at the hardware store that was covered with business cards? How was someone as inexperienced as she supposed to judge the competency of some beefy guy who claimed he could protect her?

That's why she'd turned to her brother. She *knew* he could.

"Wait," he said, relief in his voice. "I'm not using my head. One of my buddies is half an hour or less from you. I'd have tried to hook you two up, except... we're not good marriage prospects."

Despite the fact that she was desperate and in pain, Trina rolled her eyes. "I can find my own dates, thank you." Bodyguards, not so much. "Why is this guy in rural Oregon instead of at Fort Benning?" Or in some war-torn part of the world?

"IED." So casual. "Had his stays in the hospital and rehab, but he still needs some time to come back all the way. He and another friend of mine bought a ranch out there in Oregon. I think Boyd was from the area."

"They bought a ranch."

"Yeah, thinking of the future. You know? At best, we'll all age out."

She shuddered. Usually, she didn't know when Joseph dropped from the radar, which was fortunate. She worried enough as it was. He'd had regular deployments, but more often conducted raids in hostile territory, the kind of place where Americans were not welcome. She knew he'd been involved in international hostage rescues.

Perfect training for protecting her and Chloe, Trina couldn't help thinking. "So, do you have this Boyd's phone number?"

"No, this guy's name is Gabe. Gabe Decker. Boyd retired a couple of years ago. He might be getting soft. Gabe is deadly."

"But if he's injured..."

"He's on his feet. Even riding, he said last time we talked. Listen, I'll call him. Where are you?"

She explained that she was still at the hospital, but her practice partner was taking her home temporarily. She told him the address.

"I want you in hiding now," Joseph said, with the

cold certainty of a man to whom her current troubles were everyday. "Keep your phone on, but don't be surprised if he just shows up. Be ready to go."

Okay. But wasn't that what she wanted? Well, yes, but this Gabe Decker was a stranger. Was she willing to trust him? Follow his orders, if he was anywhere near as dictatorial as Joseph could be?

Her inner debate lasted about ten seconds. Because, really, what other option did she have?

The police.

All she had to do was picture Chloe's sweet face, her freckled nose natural with her red-gold hair. No, Trina didn't trust the detectives, one of whom must have a big mouth or been careless in some other way with dangerous information.

"I'll be expecting him," she said, and offered the Doughtens' address. Only after she'd let him go did she wish she'd thought to ask what this Gabe Decker looked like.

GABE'S PLEASURE AT seeing his friend's number on the screen of his phone took a nosedive as soon as he heard what Joseph wanted. Sticking him in close quarters with a clingy woman and whiny kid, right when he felt especially unsociable. Even so, he didn't hesitate.

"Anything," he said, which was the only possible answer. "Tell me what you know."

Listening, he remained lying on his back on the weight bench where he'd been working out.

Hearing that the sister was a psychologist didn't make him want to break out in song and dance. He'd had his fill of social workers and counselors both at the hospital and rehab facility. They were positive he had to be suffering from PTSD. Guilt because a teammate had died in the same explosion. Talking about it was the answer. Reliving the horrific moments over and over being so helpful to his mental health. When he balked, that had to mean he was refusing to acknowledge his emotional response to his own traumatic injury as well as Raul's spectacular death. No chance he just didn't need to talk about it, because this wasn't the first time he'd been injured and he'd seen so much death in the past decade he was numb to it.

If this woman thought she'd fix him out of gratitude for his help, he'd make sure she thought again.

His protective instincts did fire up when he heard what had happened to the kid, followed by the cold-blooded attempt to make sure that little girl couldn't tell anybody what she'd seen that day.

"Why don't the cops have them in a safe house?" He finally sat up and reached for a towel to wipe his face and bare chest. His workout was over.

"I didn't ask for details. She sounds wary where they're concerned, at least about the primary investigator."

"Okay." There'd be time for him to ask her about her issues with the police. City, he presumed, rather than the Granger County Sheriff's Department. For her sake, he hoped the murder had happened within the Sadler city limits. The current county sheriff was a fool, the deputies, whether competent or not, spread too thin over long stretches of little-traveled rural roads. Boyd had nothing good to say about the sheriff's department.

"I'll go get her," he said, to end the call. "You watch your back."

"Goes without saying." Which of course was a lie; Joseph would be watching his teammates' backs instead, trusting them to be doing the same for him.

Still straddling the bench, Gabe ended the call. A quick shower was in order. And then, huh, he'd better think about whether there were any clean sheets for the bed in the guest room. If the kid needed a crib... no, she had to be older than that to be verbal. Formerly verbal. Whatever.

Yeah, and what about food?

As he was going upstairs for that shower, it occurred to him that he'd better let Boyd know what was up, too. He was unlikely to need backup...but thinking about the bastard who wouldn't stop at anything to save his own skin, Gabe changed his mind.

Having backup would be smart.

SOMEHOW, SOMEWHERE, TRINA found a smile for Vicky, who had been fussing over her ever since Josh left the two women and Chloe at the house while he went to work.

"I'll have Caroline cancel all your appointments

for today and tomorrow," he'd assured her. "With the weekend, that gives you four days to figure out what you're going to do."

Trina hated the necessity. It was bad enough when your patients were adults, but when they were frightened, withdrawn children? They wouldn't understand.

Now she said to Vicky, "Thanks, but I'm fine." More fine if she could take the prescribed pain pills, but she didn't dare, not if she were to stay alert. If somebody had been watching the small hospital, he wouldn't have missed seeing her and Chloe leaving with Josh. Following them would have been a breeze. She'd asked Vicky to pull the drapes on the front window immediately, even though she was uneasy not being able to see the street and driveway.

"You look like you might be feverish," Vicky said doubtfully.

Trina felt feverish. But she couldn't relax and let herself be miserable until the promised Army Ranger appeared to keep Chloe safe. Really, it hadn't been much over an hour since she talked to Joseph. Expecting instant service was a bit much. Joseph might not have been able to reach this Decker guy immediately. Or Decker might have been in the middle of something he couldn't drop just like that.

Tap, tap, tap.

Vicky and Trina both jumped. That knock hadn't been on the front door. They looked simultaneously toward the kitchen.

"It might be a neighbor," Vicky said after a moment, almost whispering. Trina could tell she didn't believe it. The elegant homes in this neighborhood were all on lots of a half acre to an acre or larger. Most of the wives were probably professional women themselves, not housewives who casually dropped by for a cup of coffee.

Trina would have gone along with Vicky to see who was knocking, except Chloe lay curled on the sofa. Not asleep, but pretending to be, she thought. And the tap on back door could be a diversion meant to draw the two women away long enough for someone to come in the front and snatch Chloe.

Trina heard voices, one slow and deep. Vicky reappeared, right behind her a massive, unsmiling man who took Chloe and Trina in with one penetrating glance. Her first stupid thought was, how had anyone managed to hurt this man, given his height and breadth, never mind all those muscles?

So she wasn't at her sharpest.

"Mr. Decker?" she asked.

He nodded. "Gabe."

"I'm Trina. And this is Chloe." Who had stiffened, even though her eyes remained closed.

"Okay." His voice made her think of the purr of a big cat, assuming they purred. Velvety, deep and not as reassuring as she'd like it to be. "You have anything to bring?"

"A duffel." Vicky had scrounged some clothes from her daughter's drawers, the one who'd left most recently for college, that would probably come close to fitting Trina. Better yet, she'd produced several outfits of little girl clothing from wherever she'd packed them away with granddaughters in mind. Otherwise…otherwise they wouldn't have had a thing.

"Oh!" Vicky said suddenly. "I have extra tooth-brushes. And surely I can find a hairbrush for you."

Bless her heart, she came back with both, plus a handful of hair elastics. Something Gabe Decker, with dark hair barely long enough to be disheveled, would not have.

With damp eyes, Trina hugged Vicky. She was grateful the other woman remembered not to hug her back. "I don't know what I'd have done without you and Josh."

"We'd have been glad to have you stay, you know," she said, her eyes wet, too.

"I know, but—"

Vicky nodded. She poked the brush and other things into the duffel and said, "I can carry this out."

Gabe stepped forward. "No, I don't want you out-side. I'll take that." When he saw Trina reaching for Chloe, he shook his head. "And her. Joseph said you'd been hurt."

She had no doubt his blue eyes saw right through her pretenses. "I have burns on my back." With sud-den alarm, she remembered that he'd have to renew the ointment and bandages for her. A stranger, and male. Very male. With enormous hands that would come close to spanning her back.

That tingle couldn't be what it felt like, not under the circumstances. Especially since she knew perfectly well that no touch would feel good. Despite the gauze, she'd swear the thin cotton of the scrub top was scraping her burns every time she moved. "Can you carry...?"

His lifted eyebrow mocked her question. Yes, he could carry both, and probably pile on a whole lot more. He undoubtedly did on a regular basis, come to think of it. She'd read that soldiers often packed over a hundred pounds even in the desert heat of the Middle East.

"You're not parked out in front, I take it," she said.

"No. I drove through the neighborhood to see if I could spot any obvious surveillance. Even though I didn't, I left my truck in a neighbor's driveway. Didn't look like anyone was home. We'll cut through the trees out back." He hesitated. "You need to leave your phone behind. Better if it's at your office than with you. Or here."

Trina felt a spurt of panic. Her phone was the only possession she had left. And without it...she'd be even more isolated. But she didn't argue, knowing how easily smartphones could be traced.

"Josh will be home for lunch," Vicky said. "I can have him take it."

Gabe said simply, "Good." Trina hadn't said

a word, but he seemed to take her compliance for granted.

She lowered herself gingerly onto the edge of the sofa. Standing had had her light-headed, but putting pressure on her burns was worse. "Chloe, this is Gabe. He's a friend of my brother's. He's going to carry you, since you don't have any shoes." She now did, but they were in the duffel, and they hadn't had a chance for her to try them on. Since she knew Gabe wanted to move fast, it was a good excuse.

"Hey, little one," he said, sounding extraordinarily gentle as he bent over her.

With him so close, Trina could see the dark shadow of what would be stubble by evening, the slight curve of a perfectly shaped mouth…and a white scar that angled from one clean-cut cheekbone to his temple, just missing his eye. That was an old one, she felt sure, not the wound that had him on leave. Her teeth closed on her lower lip. If he turned his head at all, they could almost—

No, no, no! Don't even go there.

The muscle in his jaw spasmed, and she held herself very, very still. Lowering her gaze didn't help, not with impressive muscles bared by a gray T-shirt. And then there was his thigh, encased in worn denim.

Maybe he'd turn out to have a girlfriend living with him. Joseph wouldn't necessarily know.

"Here we go," he said calmly, and scooped up Chloe, tucking her against his broad chest and rising to his feet. A moment later he'd slung the duffel over his opposite shoulder, and looked at Trina with raised brows as if he'd been twiddling his thumbs waiting for ten minutes. "Can you walk?"

"Yes." She jumped up too fast. His hand clamped around her upper arm, making her suspect her eyes had done whirligigs. She blinked a couple of times and repeated, "Yes. I'm fine." Slight exaggeration, but she could do this.

He studied her for longer than she liked before releasing her. "Okay."

Vicky trailed them to the back door and locked it behind them. Gabe paused only for a moment to scan the landscape, then strode toward the trees. With so little undergrowth on this dry side of Oregon, the lodgepole and ponderosa pines didn't offer much cover, nothing like a fir and cedar forest would have on the east side of the Cascades where Trina had grown up. Gabe paused now and again and looked around, but mostly kept moving. At first, she was disconcertingly aware of how silently he moved, while she seemed to find every stick or cone to stomp on. Crackle, pop… A jingle teased her memory.

She couldn't hold on to such a frivolous thought. She felt his gaze on her a few times, too, but didn't dare let herself meet his eyes. The pain increased with each step until Trina felt as if fire were licking at her back again. Sheer willpower kept her putting one foot in front of the other. She stumbled once and would have gone down, but he caught her arm again.

"Almost there," he murmured. "See that black truck ahead?"

She didn't even lift her head. He nudged her slightly to adjust her course, but without touching her back. Trina didn't remember how much she'd told her brother about her injuries.

She almost walked into the dusty side of a black, crew-cab pickup. He unlocked the door, tossed the duffel on the back seat and placed Chloe there, too. She looked tiny on the vast bench seat.

"I don't have a car seat for her anymore," Trina heard herself say. Right this second, that seemed like an insurmountable problem.

"I'll drive carefully." He buckled a lap belt around Chloe, who stared suspiciously up at him. Then he closed her door and opened the front passenger door. "In you go," he said quietly, that powerful hand engulfing Trina's elbow. "Big step up."

He didn't quite say "upsy-daisy" but coaxed her and hoisted until she was somehow in. He closed this door with a soft thud, too, rather than slamming it, and was behind the wheel in the blink of an eye, firing up a powerful engine. When she made no move to put on the seat belt, he did it for her, not commenting on her grip on the armrest or the way she rolled her weight to the side.

He backed out and accelerated so gradually she was never thrust against the seatback.

"How long?" she asked, from between gritted teeth.

"About half an hour. Do you have pain pills?"

"Yes, but…"

"Take them. Are they in the duffel?"

She nodded.

Gabe reached a long arm back, his eyes still on the road, and tugged the duffel until it was between the seats. The bottle of water he handed her was warm, but it washed down two pills.

"You okay, Chloe?" she asked.

No answer, but Gabe's gaze flicked to the rearview mirror. "She's nodding," he said quietly.

"Oh, good." She thought that's what she'd said. The words seemed to slur. Leaning her cheek against the window, she closed her eyes.

SHE DROPPED OFF to sleep like a baby, Gabe saw. That's what she needed. He was sorry he'd have to wake her up when they got to the cabin.

The little girl was not asleep. She sat with her feet sticking straight out in front of her, her arms crossed and her lower lip pouting. Eyes as blue as his watched him in the rearview mirror. Clearly, she expected the worst. He kind of liked her attitude. He tended to expect the worst, too. That way you were prepared. Optimists could be taken by surprise so easily.

Once he made it onto the highway, he could relax a little. The couple of vehicles he could see in the rearview mirror hadn't followed them from town. At this time of morning, most traffic was headed south into town, not north out of it.

He checked on the kid, to see her eyelids starting to droop, too.

Another sidelong glance made him wince. Trina's contorted position had to be miserably uncomfortable. Burns, Joseph had said, without being specific. Gabe would have known they were on her back even if she hadn't told him, since she'd done a face-plant on the window to avoid making any more contact than she could help with the seat. Twisted as she was, he saw a thickness that could only be bandages. Or, hey, Kevlar, but that wasn't likely.

Since Joseph talked often about his sister, Gabe had known they were close. Funny his friend had never mentioned that she was a beauty, or a shrink of some kind. The stories had all been from their childhood, or repeating some amusing or pointed observation she'd made about life in general, politics and shifting international alliances more specifically. She probably followed the world news with more interest than most people did because she knew her brother was bound to get involved in a lot of the messes.

Gabe wondered in a general way what it would feel like to have parents or someone like her worrying about him. Would he be as anxious to get back in the action if his death would devastate someone else?

Impatiently, he shook off the descent into sentimentality. No family, no reason to think about it.

Instead, he circled back to the beginning. Katrina Marr would be spectacular with makeup, a snug-fitting dress and heels. Face showing strain and streaked with char, hair a tangled mess and wearing sacky, faded blue scrubs and thin rubber flip-flops, she was merely beautiful. With expressive green-gold eyes and hair the color of melted caramel, she was tallish for a woman, slender rather than model-skinny, and still possessing some nice curves.

One corner of Gabe's mouth lifted. Could be this was why Joseph never mentioned his sister's appearance. He might give one or more of the guys the idea of looking her up someday while on leave.

Fully amused now, Gabe thought that was just insulting.

But his amusement didn't last long. To stay vigilant, he couldn't afford any distraction. Somebody was gunning for the cute kid who'd now slumped sideways in sound sleep—and Gabe had no doubt Joseph's sister would jump in front of the bullet to save that kid.

His job was to make sure that never happened. Plan A, he calculated: hide them. Plan B: make sure he fought any battles that did erupt. Plan C: take the bullet himself.

Chapter Three

Trina opened her eyes to a dim room. The window was in the wrong place, she saw first. Light sneaking between the slats of the blinds told her it was daytime.

Her bedroom didn't have rough-plastered walls, either. Awakening awareness of pain discouraged her from rolling onto her back. Instead, she pushed aside a comforter in a denim duvet cover and gingerly sat up.

It all rushed back. The fire, dropping from a second-story window, the hospital. Complete loss. Wasn't that what the fire chief had said? Joseph.

Gabe Decker.

This must be his home, or at least his ranch hideout. The wide-plank floor looked like what she'd expect of a log house. A closer look at the window told her it was set in a wall thicker than usual.

And then her eyes widened. Chloe!

Still wearing the scrubs, she didn't take time to use the bathroom or find her flip-flops. She rushed out into a hall and toward the staircase at the end.

Halfway down, she heard that deep, smooth voice. He was talking to someone, pausing for unheard answers. Telephone?

The vast living room was empty. She followed the voice to the kitchen, where she saw Chloe, perched on a tall stool, watching as the big, powerful man flipped a hamburger in a pan on the stove.

"Is that a yes or no to cheese?" he asked, glancing over his shoulder.

He took in Chloe's nod, then saw Trina hovering. He didn't smile; the way he looked her over was more assessment than anything. "You're just in time for dinner."

"Dinner." She was dazed enough to feel out of sync.

Chloe swung around, scrambled off the stool and raced to Trina. She threw her arms around Trina's legs and hugged, hard. That she'd regressed to being nonverbal felt like yet another deep bruise in the region of Trina's chest.

"I'm glad to see you, too, pumpkin." Trina found a smile for the little girl, who tipped back her head to look up at her. "Why don't you start on your cheeseburger while I go back upstairs and, um, at least brush my hair?" And pee. She really needed that bathroom.

"Did you see your duffel at the foot of the bed?" Gabe asked.

"No, I suddenly panicked—" She broke off. "You know how confusing it is to wake in a strange place."

His expression of mild surprise said he didn't

know. As often as he—and her brother—woke in strange and dangerous places, they probably knew where they were and why instantly, before they opened their eyes. They probably held on to the where and why *while* they slept.

"Never mind," she mumbled, and took herself back upstairs to start over again. The woman she saw in the mirror horrified her. Her face was filthy, her eyes bloodshot and her hair a tangled mess. Lovely.

Washing her face helped only a little. She dug the bottle of pills out of the duffel and took one, hoping that would be enough to dull the pain without knocking her out again. Then she tackled her hair as well as she could when raising her arms stretched the skin on her shoulders and back. Her left shoulder ached fiercely, too, as did her left hip. No, those two pillows hadn't softened her landing on the hard ground much, if at all. The doctor had warned her to expect swelling and colorful bruises.

A ponytail proved to be beyond her. Changing clothes…not yet, she decided. She craved a shower but shuddered at the idea of hot water on her back. Spot-cleaning was as good as it would get.

And once she had something to eat, she'd have to break it to the Army Ranger downstairs that he now had medic duties as well as KP.

He studied her again when she reappeared, small lines appearing on his forehead. Apparently, she hadn't accomplished miracles.

"Cheese?" he asked.

"Please."

She leaned against a sort of breakfast bar rather than trying to sit on a stool. She studied Chloe, who had made surprising inroads on her burger, which from experience Trina knew was completely plain. She wouldn't have touched the sliced tomatoes, onions or lettuce Gabe had set out, or the ketchup or mustard, either. What surprised Trina was that the three-year-old didn't seem wary of Gabe. She shied from most people, especially men, yet was happily eating food he'd put in front of her, her bare feet swinging.

"Did you nap?" Trina asked.

Chloe nodded.

"She was up for a couple of hours in the middle of the day," Gabe said, "napped again and got up about an hour ago."

Intrigued, Trina wondered how he'd entertained Chloe for those two hours. The little girl appeared surprisingly comfortable with him. "How long did I sleep?"

He glanced at the microwave. "Nine hours."

"Really?" She'd have had to be deeply asleep for Chloe to have slipped out of bed without her noticing. "I never conk out like that."

"I don't suppose you had a very good night's sleep," he said dryly.

"Well, no, but…" Her stomach growled and she pressed a hand against it. "I'm starved. I haven't had anything to eat since last night."

"I guessed. Here." He handed her a plate with

baked beans, corn and a cheeseburger on a fat bun. "Chloe declined the beans."

The little girl wrinkled her nose.

Trina kissed the top of her head. "She's at an age to be picky."

"Figured." He produced silverware, then brought his own plate over to the bar and sat on Chloe's other side, hooking the heels of his boots on a rung as if it were a fence rail.

After gobbling half her meal, Trina said, "It's been peaceful?"

He glanced at her sidelong. "Yep. We made a clean getaway."

"Yes, but… I can't be completely out of touch."

"We'll talk about it later."

Something about his tone made her wonder how two-way he intended that talk to be. Did he really think Joseph's sister would be meek and docile? Dealing with him would be easier if she could read him better, but he was so guarded she wondered what it would take to shatter his control. Something told her pain hadn't done it. In fact, he might have shored up his walls during his lengthy recuperation.

Chloe dropped her cheeseburger without finishing it. She immediately crawled over onto Trina's lap. Trina held her with her left arm and kept eating.

"I don't suppose you have any toys around?" she asked after a minute.

Gabe snorted.

"Didn't think so."

"Actually... Well, I'll look around. I said it was okay for Boyd to loan this place out to a friend of his. Ski vacation. He had a family. Don't know how old the kids were. They might have left something behind."

Chloe's head came up. She'd been following the conversation.

Unable to quite clean her plate, Trina finished eating first. "Do you have a satellite dish?"

"Yeah. Hey. Channel three has the lineup."

She'd seen the living room but not taken it in. She couldn't describe it as homey, exactly; Gabe had furnished it with the basics but not bothered with artwork or homey touches like table runners or rugs. The sofa and a big recliner were brown leather that made her think of saddles. The clean lines of the oak coffee table and single end table might be Mission style. Built-in bookcases lined one wall and held an impressive stereo system as well as quite a library. A big-screen TV hung above a cabinet that had drawers. Trina went to investigate those.

Among a good-size collection of movies for grown-ups, she found three DVDs aimed at kids: *Finding Nemo*, *A Bug's Life* and *Arthur's Perfect Christmas*. Chloe decided on *Arthur's Perfect Christmas*. Trina succeeded in getting it started and Chloe climbed onto the sofa and settled happily to watch.

Returning to the kitchen, Trina reported, "Your

renters apparently went home without a few of their movies."

He was loading the dishwasher and glanced up. "Ones she'll watch?"

How a man could look so sexy doing such a mundane task, she didn't know, but he succeeded.

"Yep."

"Then this is probably a good time for us to talk."

"Yes, except..." She nibbled on her lower lip. "I have a problem." Actually, she had so many problems they'd add up to a lengthy list, but one thing at a time, Trina decided. "I'm afraid I have to ask you to change the dressings on my back and apply more ointment. Unless you have a mother or girlfriend nearby who could be persuaded to volunteer."

"Neither."

WELL, HELL. SHE was going to half strip so he could stroke ointment over her skin with his bare hands? Might as well ask him to run his hand along a strand of barbed wire. Dangerous. He wasn't the only one conscious of the risks, either; the pink in her cheeks was from a different kind of heat.

Think of this as a medical problem, he told himself. "How badly are you burned?"

"Not that terrible. According to the doctor, mostly first-degree, spots of second-degree. No worse than a really bad sunburn. The fire didn't touch me, but while I was lowering Chloe out the window and waiting until I could follow her, flames burst through the door behind me and—" She visibly shied from the memory. "I was just…too close to it."

"Okay." He tried to sound gentle, which had the effect of roughening his voice. "How often do we do it?"

"Twice a day until it's obviously healing. Which shouldn't be more than two or three days."

Gabe thought it over. "I don't want to leave Chloe downstairs by herself. If you'll pause the movie—"

"Why don't we wait until she's gone to bed?"

Yeah, sure. Then they'd be alone, house quiet and dark around them. Her stretched out on *his* bed, since Chloe would be in hers.

He cleared his throat. "If you don't need it done sooner."

"It can wait."

"All right." Needing a distraction, he lifted the carafe from the fancy coffee maker that had been one of his first purchases after he'd had the cabin built. "Would you like a cup?"

"That would be great."

"You okay on the stool, or would a chair be more comfortable?"

"Chair."

"Hey, hold on." He left the room, returning after a minute with a heavy-duty parka. "This should give you a little padding."

He doubled it over, and watched as she sat down gingerly. Looking surprised, she said, "That helps.

Thank you. And speaking of… I don't think I've thanked you for rushing to our rescue."

Admit to his initial reluctance? Or that, on second thought, he'd been glad to have the chance to do something really meaningful? Probably not. Gabe settled for an acknowledging nod.

"I should at least call my insurance agent tomorrow."

"It'll have to wait. What phone number would you give him if he has questions?"

"But…"

"A few days is nothing, given the time it'll take to rebuild."

She finally nodded.

"I need you to tell me what's happened so far."

Looking startled, she began, "Didn't Joseph—"

Gabe cut her off. "I want as much detail as you can give me." The cops had one goal; he had another.

She glanced toward the doorway, as if to be sure the little girl hadn't wandered into earshot. "Did you read about the murders?"

Having a whole family killed, and wealthy people at that, didn't happen in these parts. The news had likely riveted just about everyone. "Yes," he agreed, "but I had the impression the cops were holding back."

"They did tell me something two days ago they hadn't admitted up until then, but my impression is that they're stymied."

Gabe waited.

Trina began to talk, starting with the request from a Lieutenant Matson, who oversaw detectives, that she work with a three-year-old girl who was the only survivor after her family had been killed. "Either she'd climbed into one of the lower kitchen cupboards herself, or one of her parents put her there. When the police arrived, the cupboard door was open a crack, and her father's body was right in front of her."

"Once she heard the intruder leave, she might have pushed it open herself to peek out," he suggested.

"Yes, but they didn't think so. She was...frozen, almost catatonic. Stiff, staring, squeezed into the smallest ball she could manage."

He played the devil's advocate. "Seeing her father..."

"The detective said he'd been shot in his back and lay facing her. She couldn't have seen the blood or... damage."

"Unless she crept out, then went back to her hidey-hole."

"I guess that's conceivable, but I think it's likelier that she never moved." Her expression shifted. "You sound like another detective. Were you an MP, or...?"

"No, we do some of the same kind of thing when we've been inserted into a foreign country and discover our intel isn't accurate. It's time you and I start thinking like investigators." He'd realized as much immediately. "If you trust the police, you'd be letting them protect you and Chloe. They offered protection, didn't they?"

"Round the clock."

"But you called your brother instead. Why?"

She made a face. "Two reasons. One is that they're desperate for Chloe to tell them what she saw and heard. They called constantly, dropped by at the office. They were impatient, skeptical. Why wasn't she talking yet? I overheard one of the detectives saying I was being too soft, that they could 'crack her open.' His words. All I could picture was a nutcracker smashing a walnut open."

Gabe winced, sympathizing with her obvious anger. He could empathize with the cops' frustration, too, but nothing justified traumatizing that cute kid any more than she'd already been.

"They didn't like it that I wouldn't tell them where I 'stashed' her during the day, while I worked," Trina continued, with unabated indignation.

"Where did you?" he asked, curious.

"Some of the professionals and staff in the building went in together, rented a small vacant office and started their own preschool, right down the hall from my office. This way, they can have lunch with their kids, pop in when there's a slow moment, be there if something happens." She smiled. "Needless to say, it's not advertised. They were happy to include Chloe."

"Smart." He mulled that over. "Okay, you wanted to keep her away from the cops. What's the other reason you don't trust them?"

"Chloe had been talking for about a week—but timidly, and she'd clam up and stay quiet for hours if I said anything that scared her. Since she was progressing well, though, on Tuesday I called Detective Risvold to let him know we were getting somewhere."

"And Wednesday night, your house was set on fire with you and Chloe inside it, asleep on the second floor," he said slowly. Rage kindled in his chest.

"I thought the timing was suggestive." Anxiety filled her hazel eyes, and her hand resting on the table tightened into a fist. Her fingernails must be biting into her palm. "Do you think I'm being paranoid?"

"No." He started to reach for her hand but checked himself. He wasn't much for casual touching, and didn't even know where the impulse had come from. "You have an enemy. Under the circumstances, it's just common sense to be paranoid."

Her relief was obvious, her hand loosening. "Thank you for saying that. There's a fine line. Until the fire, I figured the detectives were insensitive. Maybe neither of them has children. But thinking they're part of this…"

Gabe pondered that, considering it safer than focusing on his desire to scoop her up in his arms and hold her close. That wasn't like him, either. Yeah, and she wouldn't enjoy close contact right now anyway.

"Odds are against the investigators being culpable," he said after a moment. "Trouble is, unless our guy got lucky and overheard two cops gossiping in a coffee shop, that suggests a killer who has connections in the department."

"Detective Risvold wasn't happy with me when I told him his department must have a leak."

"He was defensive?"

"Maybe?" Her uncertainty came through. "Or worried because the thought had already occurred to him? I couldn't tell."

"I'd like to have a talk with him, except I don't see how I can without giving him an idea where you are."

"Where you stashed me, you mean?"

He gave a grunt of amusement. "Okay, tomorrow, I need to grocery-shop. I'll drive to Bend so nobody I've met is surprised by what I'm buying. I can stop at Target or Walmart and pick up some toys or movies for Chloe and anything else you need."

"Wouldn't it be better if I came? I could definitely use clothes and toiletries."

"No. We can't risk you being recognized." He held up a hand when she opened her mouth to argue. "You can't tell me you don't have clients who live in Deschutes County. You could be recognized."

"The odds of someone I know happening to be in the same store at the right time isn't—"

"Give me sizes." He sounded inflexible for good reason; this wasn't negotiable. He could tell she was irritated, but he couldn't let that bother him. "You hurt besides," he pointed out. "Do you really want to try on jeans?"

She grimaced.

"I'll have Boyd come over while I'm gone."

Her forehead crinkled. "Joseph didn't sound as if

he completely trusted this Boyd. He thought he might have gotten soft."

Gabe came close to laughing. "That hasn't happened." Just for fun, he'd tell Boyd what her brother said.

Her eyes searched his. "He won't tell anyone we're here?"

"He already knows. I needed to be sure he was ready to act if I called."

When Trina turned her head, he, too, realized the background voices and music from the TV had stopped in the living room. Before either of them could rise, the kid appeared. So much for everything else they needed to discuss. But maybe one day at a time was good enough, Gabe thought. The last twenty-four hours had upended Trina's life, and Chloe's for a second time.

"Movie over?" Trina asked, holding out her hand.

Nodding, the kid reached Trina and climbed into her lap. The lack of hesitation spoke of her trust.

That got him wondering how Chloe had come to be living with the psychologist who'd been working with her. That had to be unusual. He'd never had the slightest interest in building personal ties with any of the social workers and therapists who'd made him think of mosquitoes, persistent as hell, whining nonstop, determined to suck his memories as if they were blood.

And maybe that was fitting, because his memories *were* of blood, so much he sometimes dreamed he was drowning in it.

Dr. Marr hadn't yet tried to crack *him* open, but give her time.

"Let's go run you a bath," she said to the little girl in her lap. "We'll dig in that bag and see if Vicky sent any pajamas along."

Chloe's eyes widened.

Trina chuckled. "We'll find something. If nothing else, you can sleep in this top and your panties." She nudged Chloe off her lap and rose stiffly to her feet. Looking at him, she said, "I need a mug or something I can use to rinse her hair."

"Sure." He poked in the cupboard until he found a good-size plastic measuring cup with a handle.

"Perfect," she said, taking it from him. She'd reverted to looking a little shy. "Let's march, Chloe-o."

The little girl giggled. His own mouth curved at the sound. Glancing back, Trina caught him smiling, and was obviously startled. He got rid of the smile.

"This bedtime?" he asked, nodding at Chloe.

"Uh-uh!"

It took him a second to realize the protest had been verbal. "She talks," he teased.

Trina shook her head. "Now you've done it, kiddo. You won't be able to fool *him* again."

And damn, he wanted to smile.

SOMEHOW TRINA ALWAYS ended up wet even though it wasn't her taking the bath. Chloe liked waves, and she liked to splash. She did not like having her hair washed or getting water or soap in her eyes.

At home, Trina had had a plastic stool she'd bought for the express purpose of supervising baths and washing Chloe's hair. Today, she'd knelt on the bath mat. Chuckling as she bundled the three-year-old in a towel, Trina said, "As much as you love your bath, I think you're ready for swim lessons."

Chloe went rigid, panic in her eyes.

Going on alert, Trina used a finger to tip up her chin. "Or have you taken them before?"

Lips pinched together, Chloe shook her head.

On instinct, Trina kept talking, if only to fill the silence. "Maybe swim lessons are offered only during the summer." She should know, but she tended to tune out when colleagues and friends who had children started talking about things like that. Had Chloe been disturbed only because she was afraid to put her face in the water? But Trina didn't buy that. Taking a wild guess, she said, "Were you supposed to go to the pool that day? When the bad things happened?"

Suddenly, tears were rolling down the little girl's cheeks. Seeming unaware of them, she nodded.

"Were you going to learn to swim?"

She shook her head.

"Brian?" Chloe's brother had been six, a first grader.

She nodded again, her eyes shimmering with the tears that kept falling.

"Had you just not left yet?"

Another shake of the head. Trina had a helpless moment that gave her new sympathy for Detective Risvold's frustration.

But then Chloe whispered, "Brian pooked."

Pooked. "Puked? He was sick?"

She gave a forlorn sniff. "Uh-huh."

"Did you see who came to your house, pumpkin?"

Chloe buried her face in Trina's scrub top. Her whole body trembled.

Trina wrapped her in her arms and laid her cheek against the little girl's wet head. "I'm sorry, sweetie. I'm so sorry. You don't have to talk about it until you're ready. I promise."

Worried when there was no response, she used a hand towel to dry Chloe's cheeks, had her blow her nose with a wad of toilet paper, then briskly dried her and pulled the My Little Pony nightgown she'd found in the duffel over her head. "Okay, let's brush your hair."

She found no hair dryer in the drawers and thought about asking Gabe if he had one in his bathroom, but then realized how pointless that would be. All he'd have to do was rub a towel over his head. He probably didn't even bother to comb his hair.

Well, it didn't hurt anyone to go to bed with wet hair.

She'd give a lot to have a pile of picture books to read to Chloe to give her something else to think about before she snuggled down to sleep, but she had to find another way.

So she tucked Chloe in, refrained from commenting on the thumb in her mouth, and began singing softly, starting with a lullaby. She knew the words to a couple of country-western songs, a song from *Phantom of the Opera*, and ended up with Christmas carols. After the first verse of "Silent Night," she saw that Chloe's mouth had softened and her thumb had fallen out.

Trina clicked off the lamp and had turned to slip out when she saw the big man lounging in the doorway. When she got closer to him, she couldn't miss the smile in his eyes.

So she couldn't carry a tune. *Chloe* didn't mind.

He murmured, "Grab your duffel if it has what we'll need in it."

What they'd need. Alarmed by her very sexual response to that low, faintly rumbly voice, Trina took a minute to understand. Ointment. Bandages. He wasn't suggesting whatever she'd been thinking.

Trying to regain her dignity, she detoured to pick up the bag and followed him as he backed into the hall. "My room," he said, just as quietly, and indicated an open door.

The idea of taking off her shirt and pulling down her pants for him had seemed mildly embarrassing when they first met. Now her whole body flushed at the idea.

Seeing his big bed—it had to be king-size—didn't help. Faced with that bed, she was only vaguely aware of bare walls, wooden floors and a couple of pieces of plain furniture.

"This going to be messy? Maybe you should lie on a towel," he suggested, more gravel in his voice than usual. When she stayed speechless, he went into his bathroom. By the time he'd reappeared, she had set out a big package of gauze and one of several tubes of ointment a nurse had picked up at the pharmacy for her.

Gabe pulled back the covers, exposing forest green flannel sheets, and spread a huge towel for her to lie on.

She stared at it, all too conscious of him standing less than a foot away. This was the first time since she'd woken up that she'd lost all awareness of the pain.

Feeling silly, she still asked, "Um…would you mind turning your back?"

Without a word, he swung away.

Trina squirmed to get out of her scrub top. She'd been feeling the discomfort of not wearing a bra, but even if she'd had one, it would be days before she could actually stand to wear it. All but throwing herself down on his bed, she mumbled, "I'm ready." Except for baring her butt. Well, she'd let him start at her shoulders and work his way down.

His weight depressed the mattress when he sat down at her side. While he peeled off the gauze covering, she turned her head to stare at the far wall and tried to bite back groans.

He swore. "This has to hurt like hell."

"It does," she mumbled.

There was a long pause. She heard him take a deep breath...and then he touched her. Stroked her.

Chapter Four

Gabe glanced over his shoulder as he scratched the blood bay gelding's poll. "This is Mack."

Nickering, the horse had trotted over to the paddock fence the minute he saw people approaching. Gabe was hit by a pang of guilt at the thought that the gelding was lonely. Of course he was; horses are herd animals. "Not long until you're back with your buddies," he murmured in one flickering ear.

Carrying Chloe, Trina joined him at the fence. "As in Mack truck?"

He smiled a little. "Yeah. For a quarter horse, he's a giant."

Her sidelong, appraising glance was enough to stir his body in ways that could be embarrassing.

"Kind of fits you," she murmured.

He pulled a cube of sugar from his pocket and held it out. Mack inhaled it, his soft lips barely brushing Gabe's hand. "Put me up on some of the horses here on the ranch, my boots would be dragging on the ground."

Trina's laugh lit her face. Held on her hip, the kid jumped when Mack whiffled.

"Would you like to pet him?" Gabe asked. "Mack likes everyone."

He wasn't sure the horse had ever met a child, but he trusted the good-natured animal not to bite.

The little girl looked doubtful but finally, tentatively, held out a tiny hand. Mack blew on it, making her giggle, then bobbed his head.

Gabe showed her how to offer a sugar cube, wrapping her hand in his so she wasn't in any danger of having a finger mistaken for a treat to be demolished by big yellow teeth. Another giggle, this one delighted, caused a strange sensation somewhere under his breastbone. It wasn't only Trina who awakened unfamiliar feelings. He excused himself on the grounds that he was a natural protector. The little girl's obvious vulnerability—and her surprising strength—spoke to him.

Bad enough letting the kid get to him. Gabe tried not to look at Trina, too sexy even in a pair of jeans from her friend's daughter that she was still wearing instead of the slimmer-fitting ones he'd bought her. Given her burns, the loose fit was more comfortable, she'd admitted.

He hadn't liked leaving the two of them alone yesterday, but he was confident enough that no one could find them to set out on his errands without having alerted Boyd. She'd promised to stay in the cabin and not answer the door while he was gone. Far as he could tell, she'd obeyed. He hadn't had to worry about Chloe; she stuck close to Trina.

Didn't mean Chloe wasn't getting whiny by the time he returned. Three short, animated videos only had so much entertainment value. The toys and games he'd bought had filled the evening, but he'd suggested the walk this morning to head off either Trina or Chloe growing restless.

Gabe's top priority yesterday had been to call Detective Risvold using a cheap phone he charged in his truck.

"Where the hell are they?" the detective had demanded. "Dr. Marr knows better than to disappear with the girl."

Gabe said only, "Safe. Trina asked me to let you know."

"That's unacceptable!" His fury seemed over the top. "This child is a witness to a multiple homicide. Now that she's talking, we need to have access to her. If I have to ask for a subpoena—"

"Do that," Gabe said icily, "and this is the last time I give you an update. And just how do you intend to serve your subpoena, even assuming you can find a judge who thinks it's fine to bully a three-year-old?"

After a significant pause, Risvold snapped, "I haven't heard any update."

"I'm tasked with telling you that Michael Keif was supposed to be alone that morning. The boy had a swim lesson. You can check, but chances were he'd had lessons the previous few Saturdays. That day, the mother intended to take him and Chloe. Brian got sick—puked, according to Chloe, so they made a last-minute decision not to go."

This silence lasted longer and was, Gabe hoped, more thoughtful.

"The killer was surprised by the wife."

"He didn't intend to kill them," Gabe agreed, "may actively not have wanted to, but if the husband was already down when he realized they weren't alone in the house…"

Sounding churlish, the detective grumbled, "If she can tell us that much, she can tell us what she saw."

"No. She broke down after telling Trina that much."

"I have a message for Dr. Marr," Risvold said in a hard voice. "I expect to hear from her daily. If she doesn't show up to work Monday, I'll have to assume she's kidnapped the girl and may even have crossed state lines."

The jackass was trying to intimidate the wrong man. The wrong woman, too, but Trina wasn't here. "You might recall she has legal custody," Gabe said curtly. "Which gives her the right and obligation to keep her foster daughter safe."

"Every day," the detective repeated. "I expect to see her in person, or hear *her* voice on the phone."

Shaking his head, Gabe cut off the connection. Scanning his surroundings in the vast Walmart parking lot, he saw nothing of concern except a marked

Bend PD car slowly moving two aisles away from his truck. Probably coincidental, but why take a chance?

He'd backed out, rolled down his window when he saw a trash can, dropped the phone in and peeled off the leather work glove he'd worn to handle it. Still watchful but relaxed, he had continued with his errands, the most painful of which had been choosing toys. New experience, he'd told himself. It didn't take experience to steer him away from anything battery-operated that made noises.

Gabe had been both relieved and damn glad to walk in his door at the ranch, especially since woman and girl both pounced on him with open pleasure. Hair conditioner! Lip gloss! Picture books! He'd felt kinda like Santa Claus.

Now he found a smile for Chloe. "Would you like to ride Mack?"

Her eyes widened. *"Me?"*

"If Trina says it's okay." He shifted his gaze to her fine-boned face and big green-gold eyes.

She bit her lip. "Are you sure…?"

"Mack is gentle as a lamb." He didn't remind her how a well-trained cutting horse could move—sliding stops that would send unprepared riders sailing over his head, turns faster than seemed possible for such a big animal and blazing speed for the short distances needed to run down a breakaway steer. "I'll put her up in front of me."

Amusement in her eyes, she pouted. "You didn't offer me a ride."

The words were no sooner out than fiery color rose in her cheeks. He swallowed and tried not to think about how much he wanted to take her for a ride—preferably in his big bed upstairs. Even so, Gabe had no doubt she saw the glint in his eyes, because she turned her flaming face away to kiss the top of Chloe's head.

"I was being considerate," he said. Hearing the grit in his voice, he cleared his throat. "Don't think you're ready to be up on a horse when he breaks into a trot."

Trina winced. "You're right. I'm definitely not."

Curious, he asked, "Do you know how to ride?"

"Oh, sure." Her cheeks were still pink, but she was regaining her aplomb. "Nothing fancy, just trail riding. I have a friend whose husband has a small ranch south of town. I ride with her regularly."

Good, he thought; in a pinch, he could throw her and Chloe up on Mack and send them cross-country while he held off any threat.

He put a bridle on the gelding to reassure Trina, even though it wasn't necessary. Gabe could control Mack with his legs and subtle shifts of weight. Then he used the fence to mount bareback, and held out his arm. "Ready, little one?"

Chloe was clearly torn between terror and temptation. When Trina lifted her high enough for Gabe to close his hands around her waist, she froze.

"No?" he said.

Mack had been standing as still as a statue, but now he turned his head to look inquiringly. When he blew air out through his lips, Chloe gulped and said a brave, "Yes."

The minute he settled her in front of him, she clutched fistfuls of wiry black mane. She was ridiculously tiny atop the powerfully built horse. Gabe smiled, wrapped his right arm around her and signaled Mack to walk. They circled the paddock a couple of times before he bent toward her ear. "Lope? It's lots faster," he warned.

"Uh-*huh*!"

Mack responded to Gabe's tightened legs; after one bumpy stride the horse reached a canter, the gait slow and easy, his head low. He could have been circling a show ring.

Chloe squeaked and stiffened but quickly relaxed. By the time he slowed Mack to a walk and then to a stop at the fence right beside Trina, the little girl's body was moving with the horse like a pro. She was a natural.

She beamed at Trina. "I *like* fast."

Gabe laughed, drawing a startled look from Trina. Almost…fascinated.

He was working at locking himself down when he heard a sound that instantly sobered him. The steady beat of hooves. Even Trina swung around. If he hadn't suspected who was coming, he'd have reached for the handgun tucked in his waistband at the small of his back, hidden by his denim overshirt.

He recognized the horse before the man. Gabe let go of his battle-readiness. His friend and partner rode toward them on a dappled gray. Gabe preferred quarter horses, but Boyd liked Arabs and Arab–quarter horse crosses. This one had to be a cross, tall and muscled enough to carry a big man, but still possessing the delicate ears and dished face that characterized Arabians.

Boyd's eyebrows rose at the sight of Gabe on horseback holding a little girl in front of him. A girl, he realized uncomfortably, who was wearing pink overalls and a white T-shirt that had a glittery unicorn on the front. He'd bought the damn outfit himself yesterday. Not something he'd admit to Boyd.

His friend reined his horse in and openly studied the threesome before smiling. "Gabe." He nodded. Looked at the girl. "Hi, Chloe. I'm Boyd. A friend of Gabe's." Then he let his smile deepen for Trina. He had a way with women. "And you have to be Joseph's sister."

She smiled back. "I might take insult if you tell me I look like Joseph."

Boyd grinned. "*I'd* take insult if you told me I look like Joseph." Then he considered her, feature by feature, and admitted, "There's something. Your eyes. Hair color. Otherwise…nope."

"You should have told me you were coming," Gabe interjected. He never liked surprises, and especially in the middle of a mission. Which this was, if an off-the-books one.

Boyd shrugged. "Impulse. Thought I should meet your guests."

"We were about to have lunch," Trina said. "You're welcome to join us, if you'd like."

The other man did have the grace to glance at Gabe, whose instinct was to keep even his best friend far away from Trina, but had to dip his head. They were friends, he reminded himself. There was no reason to feel territorial.

Boyd grinned, seeing right through him, and said, "Sounds good."

While Boyd dismounted and unsaddled his horse, Gabe handed Chloe off to Trina and slid off Mack. By the time he had removed the bridle, Boyd had heaved his saddle from the horse's back to the top rail of the fence and was leading the dappled gray through the gate. After taking off the bridle, too, he whacked his gelding on the butt, sending him into the paddock to join Mack.

The two touched noses, snorted and wandered companionably away to find a fringe of grass they could tear at.

Trina set Chloe down and said, "Lunchtime, sweetie."

"Can I have a cookie?"

"After lunch," Trina agreed, laughing when the kid raced toward the house.

Chloe wasn't the only one who'd been thrilled when Trina started baking last night. Chocolate chip cookies first, followed by cinnamon rolls. Two hefty cinnamon rolls had made a great breakfast this morning.

Trina, who had split one with the little girl and still not finished it, had watched him eat in astonishment.

"So, Gabe tells me your brother thinks I've gone soft," Boyd remarked.

She tipped her head to assess a man who was as tall as Gabe, but leaner. "Maybe I should send him a picture so he can see that you don't have a beer belly yet."

He laughed as if that was the funniest thing he'd ever heard. "Why didn't he ever tell me his sister was right here in Sadler?"

"Maybe because he didn't want you anywhere near her," Gabe suggested.

Boyd thought that was funny, too, possibly because he'd heard the edge in Gabe's voice.

"I'll have to call to give him a hard time," Boyd continued.

"He's away," she said softly. "That's why he asked Gabe to help."

"Yeah, so I hear." He laid a hand on her shoulder and squeezed. "Joseph can take care of himself, you know."

Her smile was obviously forced. "I do know."

Gabe didn't like seeing the shadow darkening her eyes. Yeah, being the one left behind would be a bitch. He should consider himself one of the lucky ones, knowing he wasn't hurting people who loved him, leaving them scared out of their skulls every time he went wheels up. And it would be even tougher for a lover—a wife—than it was for parents or siblings.

He had a feeling Boyd was thinking the same when he changed the subject. "Cute kid."

"Yes." Trina's gaze followed his to the front porch, where Chloe jumped from the top step to the ground, then climbed up and did it again. "She's doing amazingly, considering. Um, Gabe did tell you?"

"Yeah." Boyd's tone was grim. "No place is completely safe, but...damn."

Inside, Gabe heated the soup while Trina put together sandwiches. Two days, and they'd already begun to work around each other in the kitchen as if they'd been doing it for years, he thought, watching as she spun past him to get plates and bowls down from the cupboard. He nodded thanks and caught Boyd's interested gaze. *Like that, is it?*

No. Yes. Even if the conversation had been aloud, he wouldn't have known how to answer. He'd like to get this woman into bed—but he also knew she threatened him on a bone-deep level where he didn't want to go. If he were smart, he'd keep his zipper up and his hands to himself...except he'd be putting those hands all over her long, slim torso and the sweet curve of her ass again this evening. Even purple-and-black bruises, red skin and blisters had failed to shut down his libido.

It was like forcing an alcoholic to guzzle a shot glass full of whiskey twice daily.

During lunch, Gabe discovered something about himself, though. He didn't like the charming smiles Boyd directed at Trina, or their witty byplay. His only salvation was the slightly shy way she kept an eye on him, Gabe. It reminded him of the way Chloe watched her. Trina was the kid's anchor, and he was apparently Trina's. Then there was the fact that she never blushed for Boyd. She was being friendly, no more…which made Gabe realize that he and she never had a conversation that *wasn't* more.

Whatever this was sizzling between them, it was definitely mutual. The understanding was worrisome, even as it allowed him to relax and enjoy seeing Boyd's astonishment because a beautiful woman *didn't* flirt with him.

"YOUR FRIEND'S NICE," Trina observed, as she and Gabe stood on the front porch watching Boyd raise a hand at them and kick his horse into a canter.

"Nice, huh?" An expression that looked a lot like a smirk crossed his face, although he erased it before she could be sure.

She narrowed her eyes. "Is there something wrong with 'nice'?"

"He wouldn't be flattered. Boyd is no more 'nice' than I am."

"What's that supposed to mean?"

"Men like us…we've seen too much. Done too much."

"You're including Joseph," she said slowly.

He didn't say anything.

"So when you took Chloe for a ride, that was…?"

"Practicality. She can't tell us the scary stuff until

she's happy enough to feel safe. Besides, she'll be a pain in the butt if she gets bored."

He was that cold-blooded? Trina's first reaction was shock. But despite his current hard stare, she didn't believe he lacked any softness. He didn't give himself away often, but she'd seen fleeting expressions, the crinkle of skin beside his eyes even when he didn't allow himself a smile, a gentleness in the deep voice.

She snorted, much as horses did. "Don't buy it."

His dark eyebrows climbed. "Why not?"

"First, because I know Joseph. He…talks to me. Being a warrior and nice aren't mutually exclusive." She ignored Gabe's visible disbelief. "And I read people for a living. You know what I do."

What she'd thought was a hard stare became adamantine. Either he didn't like the possibility that she could read *him*—or he detested her profession. Needing to get it out in the open, she said, "You don't like therapists."

"You're right." He leaned toward her, letting her see something close to rage. "We're fine as long as you don't try that shit on me. You got that?"

Shaken, Trina tried to figure out why this had blown up so fast. What was he hiding?

Unwilling to back down, she nonetheless agreed. "I got it."

"Don't forget." Without so much as looking at her again, he walked down the steps and around a corner of the cabin, out of sight.

Mad more than anything, she stomped inside. Chloe sat on the sofa in the living room, clutching her plush purple My Little Pony—a gift from the jerk.

"Can I ride again?"

"Probably. Some other day." Trina found a smile. "Right now it's nap time."

"I don't wanna. I'm not sleepy."

Trina held out her hand and waited.

Chloe let out a giant sigh, slid off the sofa and took Trina's hand. "How come I hafta?"

They had this discussion daily, and Trina produced her rote answers, which Chloe countered. But Trina didn't even make it through one of the books Gabe had bought before the little girl sagged into sleep. Trina kissed her on the cheek, drew the covers up and slipped out of the room, leaving the door ajar. There she hesitated, grumpy enough she'd have joined Chloe for the nap if she'd really thought she could sleep.

Finally, she went downstairs, hoping Gabe hadn't returned. The house was quiet, so she made herself a cup of tea and curled up at one end of the sofa with it and the book she'd picked out yesterday morning.

He eventually did come in the front door, glance at her and nod brusquely, and go to the kitchen. That was the last she saw of him until long after Chloe woke, bumped down the staircase on her bottom and wanted to play a game. Trina gave serious thought to letting him deal with dinner, but she hadn't heard any sounds to suggest he was cooking and she was hungry, so she left Chloe watching a new video and went to the kitchen.

Gabe sat at the table, his laptop open in front of him. Even though she'd swear she hadn't made a sound, his head lifted and those sharp blue eyes focused on her.

"I'm going to start dinner," she said.

"You don't have to. I can—"

"It's fine." If she sounded short, so what? And she wasn't totally playing the martyr—she'd fully planned to make spaghetti this evening. She shouldn't have sulked at all; she and Gabe didn't have to be best friends, or even like each other. He was doing a favor for Joseph, and she had no doubt he was up to keeping her and Chloe safe. Full stop.

After turning on the burner, she dumped the hamburger into the pan and got out a cutting board, knife and onion. "Do you know what happened to the garlic?"

"First shelf, cupboard to your left."

Trina found it, and began chopping. "Joseph said you were still rehabilitating from an injury. I hope having us here hasn't kept you from working out."

"No, I have a gym set up in an outbuilding. That's where I was." After a brief pause, "There's a shower out there, too."

"Oh." Her eyes began watering from the onion, which she hastily scraped into the pan with the hamburger. "You're not limping or anything."

"There's still some discomfort."

And wow, did that sound like a grudging admission telling anyone he had a weakness—*having* a weakness—probably went against his nature. Plus, she felt sure he used the word *discomfort* for what anyone else would call pain—or even agony.

Having dealt with the garlic, she stirred the browning hamburger and then turned to face him for the first time in the conversation. "Joseph said you'd been hit with an IED."

His mouth tightened, and for a moment she thought he didn't intend to respond. "Yes."

"On a trail?"

"Road. Supposedly already cleared. I was in a jeep." It was as if he was trying to reduce any drama by keeping his voice completely flat.

The effect was to distance him from her. She wondered how much of a habit that was. Whether he was truly warm and open with anyone.

"By yourself?" The minute she asked, she knew she shouldn't have. She closed her eyes. "I'm sorry. I'm just being nosy. I'm not trying to get in your head or anything like that." When she let herself look at him again, she saw his spare nod.

"Your walk is looser today." His tone was cool, verging on disinterest. "Is your back feeling better?"

She moved her shoulders experimentally and, surprised, said, "It does. Maybe we can quit with the ointment. I mean, this wasn't much worse than a bad sunburn."

"I'll take a look tonight."

Deciding she'd been as friendly as she dared, Trina stirred again and then opened cans of tomatoes and tomato sauce before starting to dice a bell pepper.

Behind her, he said, "I didn't offer any way for Risvold to get in touch with you. I wonder if we should set up a conduit. Maybe one of your partners."

She shook her head. "I can call when I'm at the office."

"And just when do you plan to be in the office?" The question was lethally soft.

Trina bit her lip and turned slowly. "I've been meaning to talk to you about this."

He rose to his feet. To remind her he was bigger? Or because tension translated into action for him? "You don't want to stay in hiding?"

"No, it's not that." It was hard to argue with someone who appeared so unreceptive. But ultimately, the decisions were hers. He was a bodyguard, not the boss. "I work with traumatized children. Ones who've withdrawn like Chloe did, or are acting out in disturbing ways. These are children who have seen something horrible, or been abandoned over and over. I knew you wouldn't like it, but I can't do the same to them."

He only stared with those vividly blue eyes. "I cannot believe you're even thinking about going to work."

Trina bristled. "Thinking? I *am* going to work Monday morning."

"And if I refuse to take you?" With crossed arms, that big solid body and an implacable expression, he was letting her know the decision *wasn't* hers. "How do you plan to get there?"

Chapter Five

Still pissed Sunday evening, Gabe leaned a shoulder against the wall outside the guest bedroom as he waited for Trina. If he'd tried, he could have heard what she was reading to Chloe, but he let her voice form background music. Funny, he thought, that she had such a beautiful voice, at a lower range than most women, and yet couldn't carry a tune.

He couldn't believe that she'd won the argument. He had crumbled like a soda cracker under minuscule pressure, agreeing to deliver her to work Monday morning and pick her up at the end of the day. They had divided on whether she should take Chloe with her. If that happened any of the days this week, he'd either stay in the building as security or kill the day in town. An extra round-trip would up the risk unacceptably.

One thing he hadn't told her was Risvold's insistence that she show up daily in her office. For one thing, Gabe didn't believe the detective would get anywhere trying to slap her legally. For another...he refused to tip the scales the wrong way on this argument.

The one he'd just lost.

Man, down the line Joseph was sure to hear his good buddy had condoned and participated in this sterling plan. Gabe expected a fist in his face at the very least, since he wouldn't be able to duck her brother forever. But damn it, her argument had been persuasive. She worked with a lot of kids like Chloe, and she'd be letting them down if she had to cancel appointments for the foreseeable future. Imagining a dozen scared, mute little kids with maybe some freckles like Chloe's, and he was sunk.

He'd thought of a new argument, though, which he planned to present while he inspected her burns.

Only silence came from the bedroom now. Gabe straightened from the wall. She wouldn't go to bed without talking to him first, would she?

But no, she slipped quietly into the hallway. She jerked at the sight of him only a few feet away. But she lifted a finger to her lips, said, "Shh," and pulled the door almost closed. When she turned back, he gestured toward his bedroom.

After a noticeable hesitation, she entered it. The moment he closed the door, she said, talking a little too fast, "I really don't think you need to do this. I'm thinking I should just peel off the gauze and give my back some air."

Gabe shook his head. "You can't see the damaged skin. I can. You don't want to get an infection, do you?"

She hovered beside his big bed, not wanting to give in, but obviously unable to dispute his logic. At last, she huffed. "Oh, fine."

He couldn't have said whether he was relieved by her surrender, or dismayed. Because he knew—or at least thought he knew—why she was opposed to getting seminaked with him.

This morning, after changing her dressing, he'd been so aroused he'd had to hide out for half an hour before he dared rejoin her and Chloe. Right now... he looked down and grimaced. Sitting wouldn't be comfortable.

He hated thinking she might be uncomfortable not because she shared the intense attraction, but because she'd noticed his body's response to her.

This was probably the last time he'd have to do this, Gabe reminded himself. *Get it done.* He grabbed the towel from the chair where he'd tossed it and spread it out on the bed.

She lifted her T-shirt over her head, exposing the sheets of gauze covering her slim back, then unbuttoned and unzipped her steel blue chinos before lying down on her face.

Wincing, he sat beside her, able to adjust himself because, as usual, she had turned her face away. He peeled off tape, hating to know he was causing her involuntary quivers or see the red marks the blasted tape left behind on her creamy skin.

"Your upper back is still red, but looking good," he reported. "Not peeling yet. I don't know if aloe vera stains, but we could switch to that and skip the bandages here."

"Please."

He wished he couldn't see the plump side of her breast. Or maybe he wished he could really see her breasts, instead of having to resort to his imagination.

Gritting his teeth, he tore off more tape, eased more gauze away from her skin. Kept going until he could see the upper span of her buttocks and the curve of her hip, where the most severe burns had been. Blisters were still visible, some deflated, but a couple had burst.

"We need to keep ointment on here—" he squirted some on, feeling her reaction to the cold. "A couple of these blisters don't look good."

She mumbled something he thought was a swear word.

"Let's see how it looks tomorrow." He gently smoothed the ointment over the whole swath of skin from her lower back to her taut ass, then unrolled gauze to cover the inflamed flesh. More tape—damn, it was irritating her skin as much as the burn had in some places. Finally, he applied aloe vera to her upper back, rubbed it in, and with a supreme effort kept his hand from continuing to stroke upward onto her neck.

"Done," he said hoarsely, capped the bottle of green goop and grabbed the mess of bandages to throw them away in the bathroom. He washed his hands while he was there, too, and shook his head at the face he saw in the mirror.

That was Joseph's sister, out there on Gabe's bed. She depended on him. If he made a move, he'd risk her feeling like he'd put a price on his help.

With a groan he hoped she couldn't hear, he scrubbed his hands over his face and went out to find her sitting on the side of the bed, loose T-shirt hiding her long, slim torso and the breasts he fantasized about.

She eyed him cautiously, making him wonder what he was projecting. "So, tomorrow."

He frowned down at her. "Something else for you to consider. If Risvold can't find you, he has no way to have a subpoena served on you, either. Once he knows you're in your office, that changes. If you're court-ordered to produce Chloe and don't, you could be arrested."

"He won't go that far."

"You so sure?"

Trina pressed her lips together, then said, "What I'd do is let him talk to her. We both know what would happen."

Gabe knew. Chloe would clam up again. "What if he removes her from your care?"

"I'd like to see him try!" she fired back. "I work with the court system on a regular basis. I know judges. I could get him squished like a bug."

Apparently, he'd tossed a spark on dry wood. And

damn, Trina Marr's fury and passion fanned the fire of his arousal, too. He forced himself to back away.

"Okay." He cleared his throat. "You win."

Her gaze had dropped to his waist...and below. When her eyes lifted to meet his again, a delicate pink color infused her cheeks. "I...what?"

He did some internal swearing. "I said, you win. I'll take you to work in the morning."

"Um... Chloe?"

There was something about Chloe. Oh, yeah. "Boyd called. He has a woman lined up to watch her. She'll be here in the morning. Boyd will check in with her during the day."

Trina nodded, but he wondered if she'd taken in what he said. "I suppose I should go to bed." But her tone wasn't firm, and she stayed sitting on the edge of his bed.

"That would be a good idea." But he didn't move, either. He couldn't tear his gaze from hers, stupid as it was to keep staring at her. He'd used up his reserves of willpower in that last retreat. What he needed was a cold shower, although he knew any effect it had would be temporary. Finally, he heard himself say her name. "Trina." Nothing more.

She rose to her feet as if he'd tugged at an invisible string. Took a step. Then another. His heart pounded so hard, he heard it. The blood it was pumping was heading south, not to his head.

She whispered, "This isn't..."

"A good idea." He knew that; no longer cared,

not with her in touching distance. Without any conscious decision, Gabe lifted his hands, cupped her cheek with one, wrapped the other around the delicate nape of her neck. He took the next step, the one that brought his body close enough to brush hers. The silk of the hair brushing his hand was every bit as thick as he'd imagined, as sensual.

"Gabe."

He couldn't mistake the yearning in her eyes for anything else. That was all he'd needed to know. Even so, he bent his head slowly enough to give her time to retreat, but instead she lifted her own hands to flatten them on his chest as she rose on tiptoe to meet his lips with her own.

TRINA KEPT SNEAKING looks at Gabe during the half-hour drive into town the next morning. He was in soldier mode—his gaze flicking from the side mirror to the rearview mirror to the road ahead. Missing nothing.

They had been businesslike this morning, hustling through breakfast, both pretending the scorching kiss had never happened. She'd dressed as well as she could, given her limited selection, and come downstairs to find him letting in a woman named Diane Jenkins. Diane's husband worked for Boyd. Well, and for Gabe, too, Trina reminded herself. Except she had the impression Gabe hadn't stepped into any role as a boss here at the ranch.

Because he doesn't intend to stick around for long. The reminder left her feeling hollow.

In her early fifties, Diane had seemed nice. "Raised three girls, one boy," she told them. "You're giving me the chance for a grandmother fix."

Chloe remained suspicious of this new person but took Trina's departure with Gabe well. Her recent day care experience had eased some of her fear of being left behind.

Diane had also delivered an aging, battered pickup truck with Nevada license plates for them to use. Trina was embarrassed not to have realized that anybody watching for her arrival or departure from her office could note the vehicle and license plates. If Gabe had driven his own truck, the cops would have had his name in about a minute. Anyone else watching might have had to jump through more hoops, but she had a feeling it wouldn't take anyone who was really tech-savvy much longer.

"Whose truck is this?" she asked finally, to fill the silence as much as anything.

He barely glanced at her. "Belongs to a young guy who just started working for us. The address on file for these plates is a rental he vacated a couple of months ago. If the cops in Elko, Nevada, are inclined to do some detective work, they could help the local PD track down Antonio, but there's no reason that would be a priority for any of them. Tomorrow, we'll borrow a different vehicle. Maybe switch out plates."

"Isn't that illegal?"

He just looked at her before turning his attention to the highway again.

No, he was probably used to doing whatever he had to to accomplish his purpose.

She went back to gazing out the passenger window to keep herself from staring at his powerful hands wrapped around the steering wheel, or the muscled, sinewy forearms dusted with dark hair, or his thick, taut thighs in cargo pants. All within reach.

Arriving at the office was a relief. Trina immediately reached for her door handle, but his "Wait" had her freezing. He came around, used his body to shelter her and hustled her into the building. He didn't relax even in the elevator, and comprehensively scanned her office once they entered it. Thank goodness, they were early enough that no patients were yet waiting, but behind the counter their receptionist, Sara Houle, stared at Gabe in astonishment and more.

Ignoring her, he said to Trina, "I'll be around. Don't go anywhere without me. Not even downstairs."

"But the coffee shop—"

He tipped one eyebrow up.

Okay, with her usual midmorning latte out, she'd make it through the day on the crap coffee brewed in their break room.

Sara was still gaping. Not until the door swung shut behind him did she blink, give her head a small shake and say, "Um. I have a bunch of messages for you. Two categories."

"Two?" Trina held out her hand for the pink slips.

"Patients, social services, et cetera. The usual." Sara gave her a pile of pink slips.

"What's the other category?"

Sara's lips thinned. "Detective Risvold." This pile seemed an inch thick. "The man is *really* getting on my nerves."

Trina rolled her eyes. "That makes two of us." She glanced at the wall clock. "I should have time to call him right now and get it over with."

"Please. Oh," the receptionist added, "your phone is in your top drawer. I charged it Friday. If it hasn't held the charge, I have my cord here."

"Thanks."

Her phone came to life without hesitation, and, from the number of bars, should hold out for the day. That was good, because she needed to take this opportunity to call her insurance agent and her parents. As she scrolled to the detective's number, Trina added an item to her to-do list: *buy new cord and charger*.

Risvold answered so quickly she couldn't swear she'd heard a ring first. "Dr. Marr?"

"Yes. I understand you've been inundating my receptionist with calls. One message would have done the job."

"Would it? You haven't stayed in contact."

"I had only the one bit of progress," she said with strained patience, "which a friend conveyed to you. We haven't had any further breakthroughs, but I promise I'll let you know the minute we do."

"I want to talk to the girl."

"Your interrogation skills might work for a gang member, but for a three-year-old?"

"You're tiptoeing with her. How do you know she wouldn't respond better to firmness?"

She wanted to say, *Firm? Get real. You're a jackass*, but settled for asking, "Do you have children, Detective?"

There was a pause. "Two. And they listened when I talked."

Gee, she'd bet he and his probably adult children had a warm relationship now. Silly cards in the mail, Facebook friends, laughter around the Christmas tree.

"They didn't see their father slaughtered right in front of them. Or hear their mother's and brother's alarmed voices, maybe screams, followed by gunshots and then silence. Dead silence."

He made a noise she couldn't interpret. "So you're set on pussyfooting around with this kid?"

"Your lieutenant came to me," she reminded him. "And not for the first time." That's right—go over his head. "There's nobody else on this side of the state with my reputation for working with traumatized children. I do know what I'm doing. Give me some credit."

"Fine," he grumbled after a minute. "You can have a little longer. But *you* need to bear in mind that three people were murdered in cold blood. Kids that age forget things fast. What if what she saw is already fading away?"

"This isn't something she'll ever forget," Trina said

flatly. "If it wasn't a deep wound, it wouldn't have terrified her into refusing to speak." She frowned. "Do I gather you have no leads?"

"I'm unable to share the details of an ongoing investigation," he said, clearly having repeated it a million times. Which he probably had. He must have that line on a continuous loop. In this case, she felt confident in translating it to mean no. "It makes me uneasy not knowing where you and the Keif child are staying. We can give you added security if we—"

"I'd tell you if I believed that," she interrupted. "Forgive me, but I don't. I feel safer with no one knowing."

Sara's voice came through the intercom. "Dr. Marr, Mrs. Thatcher and Philip are here."

"I'll be out in just a minute," she replied, then told Risvold she needed to go. She swore she'd call him daily through Friday but wouldn't promise anything about the weekend.

Standing to go out to the waiting room to usher in the seven-year-old boy who woke screaming several times a night, Trina sent out a prayer.

Let Chloe have that breakthrough. Or the investigators find the answer in another way. Trina wanted her normal life back, or at least some semblance of it.

Hand clenching on the doorknob, she closed her eyes. The weirdness of her current life wasn't really the problem. What scared her was that she was in serious danger of falling hard for Gabe Decker, and if that happened, she'd be guaranteed a broken heart.

THE NEXT TWO DAYS, Gabe spent as little time alone with Trina as he could manage without being too obvious. He felt sure she noticed, but he had no idea if she was grateful or insulted.

He'd have been in more trouble if she weren't continuing to insist on going to work. Spending all day with her, no distractions, his bed upstairs in the cabin within easy reach... Yeah, that might've stretched his willpower to breaking. As it was, he just had to deal with the complications of taking her to town and back without being followed.

If this went on, one of these days he'd run out of alternative vehicles and plates. If it hadn't been spring, when Boyd always added some extra ranch hands, Gabe wouldn't have had so many vehicles to choose from. It was lucky that the young cowboys tended to be a transient population, drifting from ranch to ranch, state to state.

Monday afternoon, he'd spotted an unmarked police car parked half a block away from the professional office building where Trina's practice leased half of a floor. He had detoured by several blocks, approaching from the opposite direction and parking in back. He'd moved her out fast and had her crouch down as he drove away, heading south into town instead of west out to the highway. Only when he was 100 percent sure they didn't have a tail did he take a winding route out to the highway.

Yesterday, he hadn't worried so much dropping her off, but at the end of the day, he had her ride with one of her partners into downtown. The guy had tapped his brakes for a brief stop to let her off in front of a coffee shop. She dashed in, walked right through and went out the back, where Gabe had been waiting.

The minute she'd buckled in, she exclaimed, "This feels ridiculous, like I've wandered into a spy novel. Next thing I know, I'll be poking a packet in a tree boll for my Soviet counterpart to pick up."

Her exasperation triggered his irritation, which he didn't trouble to hide. "The cops are watching your building morning and night. I wouldn't be so worried about them, if not for your house having been set on fire with you in it." Out of the corner of his eye, Gabe saw her chagrin and moderated his tone. "It's harder to pin down whether anyone else is watching, but we have to work on the assumption they are. Thanks to the news coverage, everyone in eastern Oregon who has read a newspaper or turned on the TV knows that a little girl is the only witness to the brutal crime that has them transfixed. You called your brother because he has the same skill set I do. Would you have argued with him, too?"

She'd apologized, and he had felt like a jackass for reminding her that denial was dangerous. He consoled himself that she felt safe with him, which was good. Not so good was that he was only one man. He had backup at the ranch, but not out on the often lonely highway.

Yeah, when Joseph got back and found out what had gone on, it would not be pretty. Gabe felt some chagrin of his own. If her brother learned that Gabe lusted after his sister? Had kissed her until his brain function melted down? Gabe imagined what he'd do to someone in his position, if Trina had been his to protect.

She was, he reminded himself. Not *his*, exactly, but he was all she and Chloe had to keep them safe.

Thursday he drove his own truck, with plates he'd borrowed from an old Blazer rusting behind the tractor barn. According to Boyd, a guy working here last year had intended to rebuild the engine and replace all four tires, but spent his earnings in taverns instead and left the Blazer behind when he moved. Gabe dropped Trina off in back of her building and tried to figure out a strategy for the end of the day.

For the morning, he parked behind a Safeway store among employees' cars, backed up to a painted cinder block wall and with the nose of his truck facing out. Then he eased his seat back and opened his laptop. He'd done some reading about the crime but hadn't really dug into it.

It was past time, he thought. His subterfuges with varying vehicles and license plates might get them through the week, but beyond that? Anyone looking for them would be getting more suspicious, smarter.

Risvold, the lead detective, was leaning too hard on Trina. That bothered Gabe. Maybe it was only that the guy thought his job was on the line, but there was a hint of desperation to his unrelenting pressure. That didn't fill Gabe with confidence. It was time he pursued this as if it was a real mission. He needed to get to know the dead man, and any conceivable players.

Gabe typed *Michael David Keif* and settled back to read.

Chapter Six

Gabe narrowed his eyes at his rearview mirror. They definitely had a tail today. He wanted to think it was a cop, because the police weren't as dangerous as the alternative, but the silver sedan was hanging too far back for him to read the license plate or see the antenna. There was always something that set aside a law enforcement vehicle from everything else on the road. The lack of any of those obvious features set off a flare for him.

He did his swearing internally. Damn it, he'd been almost to the highway, where the direction he turned would be a dead giveaway. Seeing a yellow light ahead, he lifted his foot from the gas and slowed while keeping a sharp eye on the cars waiting on the cross street. If any of them seemed ready to jump the gun... But none were. The second the light flashed red, he punched down on the accelerator and rocketed through the intersection.

Trina clutched her seat belt at her chest. "Oh, my God! What are you *doing*?"

He swung abruptly right at the next intersection, silencing her. In his rearview mirror, he saw the crossover swerve, climb the curb at that corner and turn right, too.

Midblock, Gabe did a U-turn, a fraction of an inch from scraping the fender of a parked car, and sped back the way they'd come. And...yes, he hit the light just before it turned red, making it through.

"Somebody is behind us," Trina said, looking anxiously in the mirror on her side.

"*Was* behind us," he corrected.

Multiple zigzags later, Gabe felt confident he'd lost his pursuit. Just in case, he drove a backcountry route on a narrow road that swung through thinly wooded, flat land before connecting with the highway.

Once there, he took binoculars from beneath the seat and scanned both ways before heading sedately north.

"You could have been ticketed," she said after a minute. "And then they'd have found out the license plates don't go with your truck."

"They had to catch me first."

She'd clasped her hands tightly on her lap. So tightly her fingertips dug into the backs of her hands. Because they'd have been shaking otherwise?

"You okay?" he asked.

"Fine. Just..." She lifted one shoulder. "Having someone actually chasing us kind of makes this real."

"Jumping out a second-story window with fire licking at your back didn't do that?"

Trina frowned at him. "Of course it did! I just thought, I don't know, that they'd wait until Chloe was in reach again."

He shook his head. "That might have been just Risvold or one of his minions, mad that you're hiding the kid." He didn't like the doubt he felt. "If not… whoever was involved in killing her family has to be hot to figure out where you're staying before Chloe blurts out a description of the man she saw holding a gun on her daddy."

"I keep telling Detective Risvold, three-year-olds are lousy witnesses. She might say 'The man had a mean look on his face.' And maybe remember his hair was brown. How is this going to help?"

Gabe glanced at her and decided to tell her what he was thinking. "What if the killer was someone Chloe knows? That would make her a serious threat."

She pressed her lips together. "I…sort of wondered that, too. But all this pressure from above that has Risvold in a stew might only be because Michael Keif is an important man around here."

"I've been doing some research. The guy was seriously wealthy. Open Range Electronics is one of the biggest employers on this side of the state. The manufacturing jobs make a huge difference in the local economy. Plus, did you know he sat on the county council a few years back?"

"I've been doing some reading about him, too," she said. "He chose not to run after one term, you know. He wasn't defeated."

"He resigned so his partner in the company could take his turn on the council," Gabe agreed. "Still, it means the mayor, the police chief, all the movers and shakers knew him."

"Thus Risvold's panic attack."

Gabe wasn't so sure. In fairness to the lead detective, the crime was appalling. A nice mother and child slaughtered? The media had to be pushing hard for answers.

"Do you know anything about this Ronald Pearson?" he asked.

"No more than you'd have found online," Trina said. "I haven't met him or anything. I did wonder... well."

Gabe had wondered, too. If the partners were also good friends, their families would be well acquainted. You'd think this Pearson and his wife might have wanted to take in Chloe, or at least to visit her, call regularly.

Trina shifted in her seat to look directly at him. "Do you suspect he killed Michael Keif over control of the company?"

"Undecided," he said. "We need to keep him in mind, though. What I'd like to find out is what happens to Open Range Electronics now that one of the two founding partners is dead. Was it set up so that Keif's share goes into a trust for Chloe? You know, it's equally possible that, in the event of a death, the living partner gets the whole shebang."

Trina brooded for a few miles before saying, "If

O.R.E. is doing so well, why wouldn't they both have been satisfied? From what I read, Chloe's dad was the engineer who had the original concept for their first product, and supervised engineering and operations, including manufacturing. Pearson is the public face, the one who was always interviewed, who headed distribution, the sales force."

"I saw that. I also saw some indiscreet comments made by a man named Russell Stearns, who seems to have been only a step below Keif. He thought the company could go bigger, that Keif's vision was too limited and he'd been holding them back."

She stared at him. "Where'd you find that? Did this guy really go public with a criticism of the man with the power to fire him?"

"The man who did fire him. I'm guessing Stearns thought Pearson would back him, but he didn't. Doesn't mean Pearson won't immediately offer him the job as chief operating officer. With Stearns, there'd be continuity. No learning curve. And, hey, ambition. So far, they haven't brought anyone new on board. I guess that would look insensitive this quickly."

Trina shook her head. "It's just so hard to imagine a businessman massacring a family. Looking into the eyes of a six-year-old boy and shooting him? Setting the fire to kill Chloe and me?"

"And yet someone did all those things," he reminded her.

He saw her swallow. When she said, "I know," it was softly.

Gentling his voice, he said, "We have the weekend now."

She nodded, but her fingers had locked together again.

"Trina, I think you and I need to get some answers. I don't know about you, but I've lost faith in Risvold. Instead of seriously investigating, he's got himself convinced that Chloe will tell him who to arrest."

"I've noticed."

Her tartness pleased him. He didn't like scaring this woman.

"We can't exactly go canvass neighbors, though." Now she sounded thoughtful. "Or interview coworkers. And then there's the chance the murders were about something else. Say Michael or his wife had been having an affair, maybe broke it off, and the enraged third party flipped out."

"Possible," Gabe conceded, "but remember that Chloe's mother and brother weren't supposed to be there. If this was Michael's lover, would she be up to killing the whole family?"

"Maybe, if she was surprised in the act. Besides, what are you saying? Women aren't as vicious as men?"

He surprised himself with a chuckle. "No, you're right. They can be."

"Anyway, what if the killer was the lover's cuckolded husband?"

Gabe laughed openly. "Didn't know anyone used that word anymore."

She sniffed. "I read a lot. And it's accurate, isn't it?"

"Yes, it is." He was still smiling when he reached the cabin. He braked in front and said, "Go on, I know you're—" he caught himself on the verge of saying *dying* "—itching to see Chloe."

After watching her bound up the steps and go in the front door, he drove around the side of the cabin and maneuvered until he could back into the small barn he used as a garage. Closing the doors but not locking them—there was always the chance they'd need to take off in a hurry—he walked while thinking about what research he and she could, and couldn't, do.

Nobody knew him. Could he get some people who worked at O.R.E. to talk to him? Or any of the Keifs' neighbors? It would be worth asking Trina if she happened to have any acquaintance with another one of the county council members or a spouse thereof, too. Another thought: he knew several Ranger teammates who'd gone into law enforcement after retiring from the military. The option was a common one. The one who was most potentially useful, Chad Bravick, had been a detective with the Portland Police Bureau last Gabe knew. Would he be able to think of an excuse for butting in on this investigation?

Gabe grimaced. If this dragged on, he'd ask.

He said a few words to Diane and watched her

drive away, today in her own sedan. Then he let himself into the cabin, his mood lighter the minute he heard a little girl giggle, and one particular woman laugh.

"AAGH!" TRINA WRITHED, trying to reach the middle of her back and failing. "Crap, crap, crap."

Why hadn't she thought to waylay Diane before she left? Trina really hoped she hadn't been subconsciously setting herself up to have a good excuse to ask Gabe to put his hands on her again. He'd made it plain that he didn't intend to take the kiss anywhere. Fine. She should count her blessings. It wasn't a good idea. *He* wasn't a good idea, not for her—but she wasn't all that sure she had the willpower to be the one to put the brakes on.

Grumbling to herself, she went downstairs with the bottle of aloe vera. She'd been going through the stuff like frat boys did beer. Gabe had had to buy more for her twice this week.

She paused at the foot of the stairs to watch Chloe. A video played—*Finding Nemo*, or maybe it was the sequel. Chloe had her back to the TV. With a frown of concentration, she was putting together a puzzle Gabe had bought for her.

Smiling, Trina went on to the kitchen, where Gabe was hunched over his laptop. However fierce his concentration, he lifted his head immediately. His gaze dropped from her face to the bottle clutched in her hand.

"You need some help?"

"Yes!" *Tone it down*, she ordered herself. "I'm sorry to have to ask, but I itch like crazy, and I can't reach the middle of my back."

"No problem." He rose in that effortless way he had and came toward her.

"You don't move like someone who was injured," she blurted. "Do you mind… I mean, I keep wondering…"

He cocked an eyebrow. "Where I was hurt?"

She bit her lip and nodded. "I know I'm being nosy, but I can't help myself."

He didn't look all that receptive, but he hadn't gone into lockdown, either. After a minute, he said, "I told you it was an IED." When she nodded, he went on. "The bomb blew a little bit behind me. It shattered my pelvis and flung me into the air. I hit part of what was left of the jeep when I came back down. Broke my femur."

She stared at him, aghast. "You can't exactly put a pelvis in a cast."

"No." He visibly debated how much to tell her. "I had internal bleeding," he said finally, "so the docs stabilized me and then shipped me out. I'm being held together by plates, screws, pins." He shrugged. "Not sure how much real bone is left."

"I'm so sorry. Joseph didn't say how bad it was."

"I'm alive," Gabe said curtly. He held out a hand for the aloe vera. Apparently, confidences were done.

She gave it to him, turned around and lifted her shirt. She'd taken off her bra when she got home.

"Huh. You're peeling."

"I *know* I'm peeling. This is the worst part."

"Gotten a bad sunburn before?"

"When I was an idiot teenager. I learned my lesson."

She heard a gurgle, and then the cool relief as he stroked the aloe vera on. She sighed.

"It really helps?" He was carefully lowering her shirt.

"Well, it doesn't entirely get rid of the itching, but it does make a difference." Trina composed her face before she turned around. "Thank you."

"You're welcome." He nodded toward the bottle he'd handed back to her. "How long does that last?"

"Oh, a few hours, at least."

His eyes had darkened. "So, what happens in the middle of the night?"

"I...don't know. The intense itching started today."

"You can wake me up." His voice had deepened, too, becoming darker, or maybe she was just picturing him sprawled in bed, reaching for her.

It would be so much easier if she was already *in* bed with him.

Bad idea, remember?

"Trina," he said huskily. The heat in his eyes held her in place. "You have to know I'm feeling things for you. That I want you."

Dodging the conversation appealed to the coward

in her. Because her alternative was to throw herself into his arms. It was a struggle to find the in-between. "I'm…not very comfortable with short-term."

A nerve twitched on his cheek. "I've never done anything but," he admitted, in the voice that felt so much like the calloused touch of his hands.

Saddened despite her own turmoil, she asked, "Why?"

He kept staring at her, but she felt his retreat well before he rolled his shoulders and stepped back. "That the woman talking? Or the psychologist?"

What amounted to an accusation stung. "The woman. And being an Army Ranger isn't an excuse. Even Joseph has had some relationships that got serious."

Gabe gave a mirthless laugh. "Joseph would kill me if he knew what I'd suggested to you."

"You're *afraid* of my brother?" she said incredulously.

"Not afraid. Respectful."

"Respectful?" Worse and worse.

"There's an unwritten rule. Your friends' sisters are taboo."

The mood had seriously dampened, at least as far as she was concerned. "That is so ridiculous. And you're just dodging my question."

"Your question."

Oh, he knew exactly what she was talking about. "Why you never actually care about women."

His whole face tightened. "I didn't say that."

"You sleep with them, you walk away. No harm, no foul. That does not suggest an emotional component."

Gabe shook his head in apparent disgust. "You can't help digging, can you? Let's forget about it, okay?"

"Fine!" Her heartburn wasn't from dinner, but if she didn't admit he'd hurt her, it wasn't true. Right? "I need to spend some time with Chloe. Try to get her to open up a little more."

"Have you been trying at all?"

She didn't need criticism from him. "As you pointed out, I'm a psychologist. I *do* know what I'm doing." She stalked out of the kitchen, mad, hurt more than she should have been, frustrated, and suddenly sympathizing with Detective Risvold.

If Chloe would only *tell* them what she saw, this could all be over. Forgotten.

What exactly "all" was, Trina didn't let herself define.

TORN BETWEEN GOING BACK to his online research and eavesdropping, Gabe chose to hover just out of sight of the two in the living room. If Trina caught him, he was damned if he'd apologize.

"Wow!" she exclaimed. "You're a champion with puzzles."

He'd swear the warmth he heard was genuine. Frowning, he shook his head. Of course Trina was genuine. She'd stepped up to foster Chloe when she didn't need to. The trust and affection between the two of them was palpable. Why else did his chest so often feel bruised? The lonely little kid in him, the one he liked to think was no longer there, wanted in on that affection.

Pathetic.

"Do you mind if I turn off the movie? It doesn't look like you're watching it anyway."

Chloe must have nodded, because the background sound abruptly cut off.

"Come and sit with me."

He wasn't the target of that honeyed voice, but he felt the tug. *He'd* go sit with her anytime.

Some rustlings and murmuring ensued.

"I haven't been able to see you in my office in ages, so I thought we should talk now," Trina said.

For the first time, he heard the high voice.

"I don't wanna talk about *that*."

"I know. But there are other things we can talk about, too. What do you think of Gabe's house? Do you like it?"

"Uh-huh. I 'specially like his horse. Do you think he'll let me ride tomorrow?"

Trina laughed. "I think there's a good chance he'll do that."

Gabe smiled. Chloe was a really cute kid who had him wrapped around her little finger. He'd never understood the appeal of having children before, mostly seeing them whining in grocery store aisles, but she'd opened his eyes. She was sweet and gutsy.

"We'll go ask him when we're done talking. How about that?"

"Can we be done talking *now*?"

Gabe's smile widened into a grin.

"Nope," Trina said cheerfully. "Did Diane keep you from being bored today?"

"She's nice. She even watched my movies with me." It was a clear accusation. *If she will, how come* you *don't?*

"Did she tell you she really, really wants grandkids? I'm pretty sure she's practicing. After spending time with you, she'll be ready to be a grandma."

There was a pool of silence, followed by a small "I used to have a grandma."

"You still do, sweetie. She's hurting. Your mother was her daughter, you know. And Brian her grandson. When you wouldn't talk, she thought I could help you better than she could."

"But I talk now."

Trina laughed. "She knows that. I'll tell you what. Once we can quit hiding, we'll go visit her. I'll bet she'd love that."

"Okay."

"Good. So I've been wondering about something. I know you hid in a cupboard in your kitchen."

Silence.

"You remember my kitchen, right? And you know Gabe's kitchen."

He tipped his head. Where was this going?

"And Gabe doesn't even live here most of the time,

which means he doesn't have as much stuff as most of us do. So, here's my question. How come there was enough room in there for you to hide? Was that cupboard empty?"

Clever.

"Mommy took the stuff out."

"What kind of stuff?"

"Cookie sheets 'n… I don't know. Flat things."

"Ah. It was that kind of cupboard. I didn't have one of those, but Gabe does. Those are *skinny*. Lucky you are, too."

The giggle told him some squeezing was going on.

"But when did your mommy take the things out? Had she been washing them or something? She didn't leave them just sitting on the counter, did she?"

"Uh-uh. She… I think she put them on top of the pans in the *big* cabinet. It's under the stove."

"Oh, that makes sense. Whew! I kept picturing you sitting in a giant mixing bowl or on top of pans, which wouldn't be very comfy."

"Mommy made room for me."

"Did she tell you to hide in there?" Trina asked gently.

This time the silence went on so long Gabe thought Chloe wouldn't answer.

The voice that did come was Chloe's, but…different. Eerie. "Mommy said to stay and not make a sound, not even a teensy sound. No matter what I heard."

"Oh, honey." Heartbreak weighted Trina's voice. "I'm sorry. So sorry."

"And I didn't make a sound." This was a wail. "I didn't! 'Cept now I am, and Mommy said I shouldn't. Not till she came back. And she's not back! Why didn't she come back?"

The anguish in those sobs had Gabe flattening his hands on the wall and letting his head fall forward. He wanted to wrap his arms around that little girl and tell her that she didn't have to talk about whatever horrible things she'd seen and heard. That she didn't have to be afraid, because he'd stand between her and the rest of the damn world.

If his hands had been pressing wallboard, he might have damaged it. The logs were impervious.

Trina whispered broken reassurances until the sobbing eased, became snuffles and whimpers.

"Did you push open the cupboard door so you could peek out?"

Nothing.

"I think it might help if you could tell me what you saw. Sometimes saying what scared you out loud makes it less scary."

When he didn't hear anything more, Gabe shoved off from the wall and walked into the living room, the hell with staying out of sight. He saw Trina's distraught face first, then, once he rounded the couch, the child clinging to her like a baby monkey—arms and legs both gripping her, head buried against Trina's breasts.

And that's when he heard the soft keening. "No, no, no, no, no."

His horrified eyes met Trina's.

Chapter Seven

Lying in bed that night with his hands clasped behind his head, Gabe stared up at the rafters and soaring, dark ceiling. The faintest hint of light from the hall cast shadows that wouldn't normally be there.

What Chloe had told them today verified the assumption that her mother had had some warning. Had she heard her husband and another man—or maybe more than one person—shouting? If she'd heard a threat, or glimpsed someone pulling a gun, why hadn't she grabbed Chloe and slipped out the back door?

Easy answer: because her son was upstairs in bed, sick. She thought she could get him out, or hide them both. No, probably not hide him—he'd been found dead on the stairs, her at the foot of them, possibly having tumbled a distance. The police would know for sure, from blood on the steps and from her autopsy. Either way, she and Brian had been trying to tiptoe down and slip out of the house, Gabe guessed. One of them had inadvertently made a sound, or the killer had walked out of the kitchen to leave and seen them.

The sad thing was, if they had hidden, they'd probably have survived, given that the killer likely assumed the house was empty but for his target. Rebecca Keif wouldn't have had time to think it through, though. She heard an explosive argument; by the time she got her son out of bed and moving, she might have heard a gunshot. Her only thought would have been of her children, her main goal escaping with them.

After Chloe's breakdown tonight, Trina had sat with her while she took a bath. When Chloe emerged from the bathroom, he'd squatted to give her a big, good-night hug. He'd been newly conscious of the fragility of that small body. He couldn't get his last glimpse of her out of his head. On her too-pale, pinched face, her freckles had stood out like rust-colored paint splatters.

Trina had stayed with her a long time, reading and then singing. He didn't hear a peep from Chloe, who'd lost her voice again after her haunting repetition of "no."

With the night completely quiet, he heard that eerie voice again. *Mommy said to stay and not make a sound, not even a teensy sound. No matter what I heard.*

Gabe mumbled an obscenity under his breath.

He'd spent hours himself crouched in places where he was a breath away from being discovered, and his teammates' lives as well as his had hung in the balance. The creak of a floor, or a faint crunch of rocks underfoot; an involuntary sneeze, or a stomach rumbling, or a small movement that brushed the barrel of his AK-47 against sandstone—any of those would have meant death. And he was an adult, a soldier who'd gone through grueling training and survived countless missions, yet he still remembered the bowel-loosening moments when he thought he'd blown it, or that one of his teammates had. If some of those instances still lurked in uneasy corners of his mind, appeared in dreams, how much worse must it be for a three-year-old child who'd been loved and pampered, probably never knowing any real fear?

And when she emerged from hiding, it was to find she was the only survivor. Career soldiers cracked when that happened. They spent the rest of their lives asking themselves why *me*?

He stiffened at a faint noise from the hall. Bare feet brushing over floorboards. A door closing. Probably Trina using the bathroom, which meant she hadn't dropped off to sleep any better than he had. But there was a small chance it was Chloe who had crept out of bed. While on his shopping spree last weekend, Gabe had bought a plug-in night-light for the bathroom so she'd feel safe getting up in the night.

After he heard the toilet flush and the door open again, the pad of footsteps came back down the hall… and paused in front of his open bedroom door.

"Trina?" he said softly.

"I… Yes," she whispered. "I'm sorry, I didn't mean to wake you."

"You didn't. I was lying here thinking." He rolled onto his side and stretched out to turn on a lamp. "Come on in."

She hovered in the doorway, wearing boxer shorts and a tank top. All that uncovered skin seemed to glow in the diffused light. "I shouldn't. It's just…"

"You itch."

"Yes."

Tending to run hot, he'd pushed all his covers to one side and had only the sheet pulled up to his waist. She wasn't the only one exposing a fair amount of bare skin.

"Why don't you go get the aloe vera?" he said reasonably.

Her head bobbed. The maple brown hair she so often wore in a ponytail or a twist at the nape of her neck or even French braids hung loose tonight, falling below her shoulders. Once she'd disappeared, his hands tightened into fists. He had to deliberately open and flex his fingers before she came back.

Relaxed, that was him. Not so easy to project, when he was horny as hell. In fact…he glanced down his body, grimaced, and bunched up the sheet. In the nick of time. Given that she'd said a clear "No," seeing his response to her could rightly offend her.

Trina entered into his bedroom, looking shy. "Thank you."

"No problem." He sat up, leaving enough room

for her on the edge of the bed beside him. Lucky he'd taken to wearing flannel pajama pants because of his guests.

With another wary glance over her shoulder, she sat where he'd indicated and lifted the tank top, although not pulling it over her head.

Without comment, Gabe took the bottle and began spreading the goop. When he heard a small moan, his hand stilled and he had to swallow hard before continuing.

"What about lower?" he asked after a minute. "Or doesn't it itch?"

"I can reach that."

Well, hell.

"Chloe sleeping okay?"

Trina nodded, easing the tank top down before swiveling a little to look at him. "She conked right out."

"Are we back to square one with her?"

"You mean, will she talk in the morning? I think so. I hope so. Tonight she just…shut down."

"She told you a lot."

"I know. If only her mother had hidden."

"I was thinking the same. But reality is, something horrific blew up really fast and she was in a panic."

A shudder rattled Trina's body. "I know about that."

"Yeah, I guess you do." He didn't like thinking how close she'd come to dying. He knew without asking that, under pressure, saving Chloe had come well ahead of saving herself in Trina's head.

She sighed. "If she'd just tell us."

His "Yeah" came out gruff.

Her eyes searched his. "Do you think we should call Detective Risvold?"

"We just about have to, even though all she did was confirm what I'm sure the police suspected. I need to go out for groceries tomorrow, anyway. You can make me a list after breakfast."

"Yes. Okay." Her muscles tensed. "I should go to bed."

"Don't." Without a conscious decision, his hand closed around her wrist. It was an effort to keep the grip light, so she wouldn't feel trapped.

"But...we agreed."

"Did we?"

"Is this like benefits for the bodyguard gig?"

Stung, he released her hand. "You're right. Get to sleep."

After a hesitation, she stood. "I shouldn't have said that."

"It was as good as a slap in the face." He lay back against the pillows, hoping he was doing impassive better than he feared. "But I set myself up for it."

"Can't I say I'm sorry?"

Last thing he wanted to hear. "Go to bed."

Something about the quiet talk and the night and the intimacy had apparently blasted his rightful hesitation where she was concerned. He'd really thought, if he put himself out there again… Stupid, and not like him. But whatever seethed in him because of Trina wasn't usual for him, either.

Clasping her hands in front of her, she said with dignity, "I can't have fun and then shrug you off."

She gave him ten or fifteen seconds before she nodded and left.

He turned off the lamp, pounded the mattress with a fist and thought a lot of things he shouldn't be.

FRIDAY, WHILE TRINA WORKED, Gabe continued his so-far unproductive investigation.

Driving a slow path through the Keifs' neighbor-hood, he scanned the monster of a house owned by their next-door neighbors. Along with the standard attached two-car garage, it also had a separate four-stall garage. His eyebrows lifted at the sight of a red BMW in the driveway. Someone had to be home. On his couple of other forays in the neighborhood, no one had answered the door at this place.

Gabe parked as inconspicuously as possible, tucked up beside an RV beneath a high roof that extended from the detached garage. The Sadler PD might be doing drive-bys, and he didn't want either his truck or the license plate on it to be noticed.

Now came the challenge. He'd found a couple of neighbors happy to talk about the murdered family, not much caring who he was or what he represented. But he'd had a few doors closed firmly in his face, too, when he couldn't produce any convincing ID.

An attractive blonde he guessed to be around fifty came to the door.

He said apologetically, "I'm sorry to bother you, but I had some questions about the Keifs. I haven't caught anybody home here."

"What a horrible tragedy," she said without hesitation. "But I don't know what I can tell you. Jim and I already spoke to that detective."

"I'm only interested in the Keifs' routines." Gabe aimed for soothing. "People you might have seen in and out of their house."

"Well, no one suspicious! They entertained regularly, you know, and had the two darling children." Thinking about the kids noticeably hit her. "It's so hard to believe…"

When he told her he'd met Chloe and that she was doing well, the neighbor regained her poise and continued to chatter. Yes, she and her husband had gone to parties at the Keifs', and had entertained them here, too. Everybody liked them, she was sure.

Gabe showed her pictures he'd printed of Stearns and Pearson. Pearson, she recognized immediately.

"Well, they were partners, after all." Her forehead wrinkled. "Now that I think about it, I haven't seen them here in a while." But she shook off the thought. "Goodness, Ron and his wife may have been away! The other man…" She couldn't remember ever seeing him.

"The awful thing is," she confided, "I drove by their house that morning. I even glanced at it, I don't know why, you know the way you do if you see movement, but I must have been imagining it."

"Were there any unfamiliar cars in the driveway?"

"I don't know…" Her voice slowed. "I think maybe there was. That could have been what caught my eye." Appalled understanding spread on her face. "Oh, dear Lord. Why didn't it occur to me? That detective never asked."

THE WEEKEND HAD proved to be an oasis in the tension, Trina thought.

Right now, with the exception of the clop of the horses' hooves and the creak of leather, the stillness seemed absolute out here in the lodgepole and ponderosa forest. Sunlight penetrated pine branches in golden streams.

Feeling content for this short interval, Trina rode a dun mare that followed Gabe and Chloe on Mack. Although she felt sure that this mare came to life in a herd of cattle, right now Trina could have been on the kind of plodding horse used in trail rides for urban visitors experiencing the "Wild" West. Reins optional. In fact, she let hers hang loose.

Yesterday, Chloe had been…not mute, but definitely subdued. She'd perked up when Gabe took her for a ride around the paddock again. Today, apparently having judged Trina to be healed enough, he'd ridden to the ranch proper and returned with a saddled horse for her to ride.

She cocked her head when she heard Gabe and

Chloe having a low-voiced conversation, but she couldn't make out what they were saying.

The next second, he urged Mack into a lope. The dun Trina rode leaped to follow suit, startling her. She looked ahead anxiously. Did he know what he was doing? He'd been careful with Chloe so far, but—

Chloe's laugh floated behind her.

Smiling, Trina relaxed.

Gabe eased them to a walk again, and not ten minutes later, the cabin and barns came in sight through the trees.

He abruptly reined in Mack and gestured to Trina to be quiet. What... Then she, too, saw sunlight glint off the roof of a car parked in front of the cabin. One that had a rack of lights on top. A uniformed officer was coming down the steps from the front porch, his head turning as he scanned the outbuildings much as she'd seen Gabe do.

The mare started to shake her head, but Trina laid a hand on her neck to stop her before she blew out air.

After a minute, the man got back into the SUV, swung it around and drove back down the narrow lane.

Still watching it, Gabe asked, "Did you know him?"

"No."

Once the car was out of sight, they rode together to the barn. After dismounting, Trina reached for the mare's girth, but Gabe shook his head. "I'll take care of the horses. You and Chloe need to get inside."

Stress stole the relaxed pleasure of the outing. "But if anybody has been watching, they'll recognize you, too."

"Nobody will see me."

She took him at his word and led Chloe inside. She was sweating, and decided they smelled horsey. They both needed a shower, Trina decided.

Wet hair felt heavenly when she and Chloe went back downstairs to prepare lunch. Trina had cooked an enormous pile of potatoes and eggs earlier, and now she drew a stool up to the counter so Chloe could "help" her make a potato salad.

The back door opened and Gabe came in, hanging his Stetson on a hook just inside the door. His eyes met hers briefly. Then he said, "Let me go wash up," and walked through the kitchen. Footsteps on the stairs came a moment later.

Trina blinked and gazed down uncomprehendingly at the cutting board and her hand holding a paring knife. Sweaty men had never done it for her before, but, well, apparently there was an exception. As short as his hair was, she'd been able to see a line left by the hat. His angular face had gleamed, and she'd focused on droplets of sweat on his brown throat.

Oh, my.

She'd gotten a grip on herself *and* finished the salad by the time he returned, clearly having showered and changed to clean jeans and a T-shirt that fit snugly over powerful biceps and pecs.

She rolled her eyes at herself and starting slapping together sandwiches.

Just as they were sitting down, Gabe's phone rang. He pulled it from a pocket and answered. "Boyd," he said, probably as much for her sake as in greeting. Then he mostly listened, responding with occasional monosyllables.

Once he'd finished the conversation, she lifted her eyebrows inquiringly, but he gave his head a slight shake and asked Chloe how she'd liked the ride.

He was waiting in the kitchen after Trina settled the little girl in bed for her nap, a fan on a low setting stirring the hot bedroom air.

He'd opened his laptop again, but looked up the minute she appeared. "Boyd said he had a visitor. Sadler PD officer, following up on a vehicle he claimed had caused a minor accident and fled the scene."

"What? He lied?" Her surprise felt like naïveté, but as irritating as she found Detective Risvold, she had trouble believing the local police could be corrupt.

"Whoever sent him out here would have had to come up with a story that justified the time and bother."

Trina nodded doubtfully.

"Fortunately, the number he had was from a derelict vehicle abandoned here by a ranch hand moving on. Boyd assured the cop the guy had left last year. He showed him paperwork proving it, and said he'd have sworn that young cowboy had said he was going back to Montana where he'd grown up. He didn't mention that the kid had left his Blazer behind. Not much the cop could do."

"No." They were so lucky the officer hadn't been in pursuit of one of the other sets of license plates Gabe had borrowed.

"Another problem," he said, not giving her a chance to dwell on the last one. "Diane's youngest son was in a car accident last night. She left first thing this morning for Boise. She made Boyd promise to tell us how sorry she was to let us down."

Having really liked the older woman, Trina exclaimed, "Oh, no! Was it bad?"

"The accident? The boy's injuries aren't critical, Boyd says. Broken arm and nose, minor concussion." Gabe shrugged. "Kid's only twenty, though."

"And her baby. Of course she had to go."

"I guess so." He didn't sound convinced. "Boyd's looking for a replacement."

"We could take Chloe," Trina suggested tentatively. "Nobody even knows the day care is there."

"You so sure about that? If a cop came into the building and asked questions?"

That silenced her.

Was her stubborn insistence on going to work endangering the little girl who depended utterly on her? Trina hadn't been able to help asking herself the same thing often last week. But then she'd think about the children she'd be working with the following day, and would come to the same conclusion. Her first appointment tomorrow was with an eight-year-old girl who'd been savaged by a dog and was now facing multiple surgeries and living with scars. Terrified of any and all animals, she didn't want even her friends to see her. The mom had had to take a leave of absence from work because Ashley had screaming fits at the idea of returning to school.

Trina suddenly became aware of Gabe watching her, intensity in his blue eyes. "What are you thinking about?" he asked.

She told him.

He sighed.

GABE GLANCED IN the rearview mirror, seeing Chloe whispering to her stuffed unicorn, and therefore unlikely to pay attention to anything the adults said.

He made sure he had Trina's attention before saying in a low voice, "You know the plan. I want anyone watching to see you go in alone. Chloe and I will be up in a while. Day care is the last door on your hall, right?"

"Right."

He'd argued against bringing Chloe from the beginning. Once—*if*—she was spotted, he knew the killer would make a move. Probably not armed gunmen assaulting the professional building, but he couldn't rule even that out.

Trina did share his worries. The cop stopping by the ranch yesterday had made the risks they were running daily damn real, even to someone who'd been trying to bury her head in the sand.

The trouble was, Chloe didn't want anything to do with the replacement Boyd had found for Diane. The woman—girl—had stopped by the ranch yesterday to meet them. When Trina explained to Chloe that Diane wouldn't be able to come the next day to stay with her, but Kaylee would be here instead, Chloe shrank away. Kaylee squatted down to her level and coaxed, talking about how much fun they'd have. Chloe wasn't having any of it.

She'd latched on to Trina's leg and refused to let go. She didn't want to watch a movie, or play, or look at her books. The rest of Sunday, she followed Trina everywhere she went, even waiting outside the bathroom door.

He had a suspicion she hadn't objected to Kaylee, but rather to one more change. And she wasn't about to give up.

First thing this morning, she'd started whimpering. "I wanna go. Why can't I go?"

On about her twentieth teary repeat of "Don't leave me. Please don't leave me," Gabe had relented, but he remained on edge.

He'd tried reasoning with himself. If anyone was watching for Trina, they'd see her go in. Why would they hang around to notice some man bringing a child in later? Between the psychologists and doctors with offices in this building, kids came and went constantly.

Screw reason. If he'd been the hunter, he'd have

eyes on this building all day, every day when Trina was at work. Front and back. He wouldn't let denim jeans, plain T-shirt and a kid-sized baseball cap fool him into thinking this particular child was a boy.

Trina had worried about the lack of a car seat, but since Chloe would then sit higher, she'd be a lot more visible using one. They couldn't afford that. In fact, as traffic became heavier, he said, "Okay, kiddo, time to lie down."

Chloe obligingly lay down sideways on the seat. This was a game to her.

Thank God, she didn't throw a fit when Trina got out in the back of her building. Instead, she waved bye-bye without apparent alarm. Gabe had no idea how a kid's mind worked, but he was thankful she considered him to be safe. Her trust actually gave him a little bump in the chest, but he wouldn't have admitted that to anyone.

He drove a winding route through town watching for a tail, but not identifying one. Finally, he parked several blocks from Trina's building, put on a black Stetson and got out. He'd come in disguise today, too: black dress slacks, a crisp white shirt and shiny black cowboy boots. A Western-cut jacket hid his gun. The Stetson would make it more difficult to get a good look at his features. Then, after nixing the purple unicorn, he carried what appeared to be a little boy casually along the sidewalk and walked right in the front door. Father bringing his kid to an appointment.

Well, he got Chloe to her day care safely. He even texted Trina to let her know.

His real fear was how they'd get her *out* unseen at the end of the day.

Good thing he had plans to keep him busy today.

CLOAK-AND-DAGGER STUFF was so not for her, Trina realized, as she clutched Chloe close and squeezed between bodies so that they'd be initially hidden when the elevator opened. She could get a look at anyone in the lobby and, if she saw something worrisome, maybe take some kind of evasive action. She'd made sure to get on an elevator with several other parents who'd also picked their kids up at the day care, plus one unknown woman carrying a baby, probably after a visit to the pediatrician on the same floor.

The elevator lurched and the doors opened. Her pulse raced, but nothing obvious leaped out at her, so she hustled toward the back exit that led into the parking lot.

Of course Gabe had been watching for her, because the black truck roared right up, only feet from the door. Some people looked annoyed, having to circle around it, but she jumped into the back seat with Chloe and said, "Go!" even as she was buckling the seat belt around the little girl.

As planned, she stayed in the back seat, keeping a hand on Chloe, who was once again lying down. Her own gaze roved anxiously, even as she saw that

Gabe's flicked unceasingly from the road ahead to each mirror and back again.

He drove a different, meandering route through town each day. Usually, she sensed some relaxation, but today he seemed tense.

"Is everything okay?" she asked.

"I don't know."

That was it. *I don't know.* Her fear ratcheted up.

Eventually, he did turn onto the highway, driving fast. The landscape blurred. It felt as if he was accelerating.

Then, suddenly, he said, "Hell. This is an ambush. They're coming up behind, and someone is waiting up ahead for us."

Her teeth wanted to chatter, but she refused to surrender to that kind of cowardice. "What do we *do*?"

His lack of an immediate answer *was* an answer.

The locks snicked. Their speed climbed.

Chapter Eight

"You and Chloe stay down," Gabe said, keeping his voice level. "Do *not* raise your head for any reason. Do you hear me?"

"Yes."

He opened the glove compartment and removed his SIG Sauer. It fit comfortably in his hand.

Trina must have seen him, because she sounded shaken. "Isn't it likely this is the police?"

"No. If it was, they'd have had no reason not to turn on flashers and pull me over back in town. Aside from refusing to disclose Chloe's whereabouts, you and I have been cooperative. Stayed in touch, passed on what we'd learned."

"Yes. Oh, God. What are you going to do?"

"We'll see."

He couldn't lose focus enough to comfort her. A car had just sailed past going south. In seconds, it would be out of sight. Otherwise, the highway was empty in both directions but for the obviously powerful dark sedan closing the distance on his truck from

behind—and the big black SUV that had been waiting on the shoulder ahead, but was now moving. To
make a U-turn? No, it had pulled across the highway
to form a barricade.

Son of a bitch. He'd almost called Boyd earlier and
asked him to make the trip to town so they'd have an
escort home. *My mistake*, he thought coldly.

The sedan was close enough that he could see it
carried a driver and passenger. He'd count on at least
two men in the SUV, too.

He'd begun slowing down, as if he didn't know
how to handle this. Braking. The broadside SUV
reared ahead.

"All right," he said harshly. "Down. Both of you
on the floorboards."

Chloe's squeak of surprise came from behind him,
but the click of the seat belt and rustlings let him
know Trina was doing as he said. When he took a last,
hasty look behind him, he saw that she was lying on
top of Chloe. Using her own body to protect a child
who didn't deserve any of the crap that was happening to her.

A man had stepped out of the SUV and was wav-
ing his arms, signaling Gabe to stop. Looked innocent enough…if the guy hadn't made the mistake of
leaving his door open, allowing Gabe to see the rifle
aimed right at him.

"Trina, I need you to memorize a license plate
number." He didn't wait for any assent, reading off
the one displayed on the sedan closing in on them.

He lowered the passenger-side window, waited until the SUV was no more than thirty feet ahead and the sedan was braking—and then slammed his foot down on the gas pedal while yanking the wheel sharply to swerve toward the far shoulder.

The man standing, exposed, leaped back, momentarily blocking any shot from the gunman.

Time slowed, as it always did for Gabe in combat. There was an almost surreal clarity. The tumbleweed and sagebrush land to each side of the highway could almost have been Iraq or Afghanistan.

Judging his moment, he took his first shot out the passenger window. Back tire.

Still coldly, without compunction, he fired at an angle into the windshield. Out of the corner of his eye, he saw a web form in the safety glass…and the gunman slumping to one side.

Then he accelerated, the left wheels off the pavement, tilting the truck. Metal screamed as he scraped the passenger side against the SUV bumper.

Same color paint jobs, he thought, in that strange way one did. In the clear, he braked briefly, long enough to take out another tire—and to ping a bullet off the sedan.

It rocked, swerved, the driver losing control. The left side crumpled as it came into hard contact with the bumper. But—hell!—it was still in pursuit.

Gabe had a head start, though, and he'd halved the enemy. Rocketing down the highway, he set his weapon down on his seat long enough to grab the phone and speed-dial.

"Got a problem," he told Boyd.

MINUTES LATER, THE SEDAN, built for speed in a way the truck wasn't, once again closed in on his bumper.

Two more minutes, he told himself. One…

His back windshield exploded and he heard a thump.

The hair on the back of his neck rising, he swerved, driving in an unpredictable zigzag pattern that would make it hard for a gunman in an also-moving vehicle to make an accurate shot. The big tires squealed. A bullet pinged off metal. Tailgate or fender. Son of a bitch. The Ford F-250 was almost brand-new.

Up ahead, another pickup truck waited on the shoulder. He was almost on top of it before he was able to see the man crouched low in the bed, rifle barrel resting on the tailgate. Just as he flew past, he heard the crack of the rifle. Once, twice, three times.

The sedan spun in the middle of the highway, skidded toward the embankment…and plunged over.

In seconds, Boyd's truck fell in behind Gabe's. The turnoff was several miles beyond. He took it carefully, slowed to a near crawl. A cloud of dust would have been a dead giveaway.

"You okay back there?"

"Yes." Trina was breathless but didn't sound panicky.

"You can get up now. We're almost home."

Home. The word felt like an unexpected speed bump. Despite his investment in the place, he'd never thought of the cabin or ranch as "home." But he didn't let himself dwell.

"Did I squish you?" he heard her ask Chloe. He didn't take in the response, but relaxed when he saw them both pop up and take their seats. Trina didn't even reach for the seat belts, obviously recognizing where they were.

Boyd stuck with him when he veered right at the Y, following him behind the cabin but giving him room to maneuver so he could back into the outbuilding, as always.

Gabe unlocked the doors, using the moment when Trina got out carrying Chloe to slip his gun into his waistband at his back. He tugged the white shirt out to disguise it and followed them.

Boyd was already waiting. Leon Cabrera hopped out of the bed, landing lightly on his feet. No sign of the rifle.

Trina smiled at them. "Thank you for…for coming." She looked down at Chloe, resting her on one hip. "You remember Mr. Chaney, don't you?"

Chloe buried her face.

"Trina Marr, meet Leon Cabrera. He's another retired Ranger. I'm sure Joseph would remember him. I was lucky enough to talk Leon into coming to work here as our foreman."

Leon happened also to be a trained sniper as well as unflinching in action. Lucky he'd been readily available, although Boyd had tried as much as possible to hire people with a military background. Made the ranch damn near impregnable, although neither he nor Gabe had ever expected to have to defend their property.

"Come on in," Gabe said. "You've got time for a beer, don't you?"

"Sure." Boyd sounded as if this were a casual stop by to say hey.

Inside, Trina got out a tin of the cookies she'd baked and plopped it in the middle of the table, then poured milk for Chloe. The two left the room. The men didn't say much until they heard the TV come on in the living room.

Finally, Boyd said quietly, "Whoever this is has an army."

Trina returned to the kitchen and sank down in the fourth chair at the table. "Tell me what happened."

Realizing how blind and helpless she must have felt, Gabe gave her a quick summation.

She stared at him. "Did you kill anyone?"

"I don't think so." At this point, he wasn't sure he cared if he had, but he didn't say that. "I winged one of them. Shot out a couple of tires."

"That's what I did, too, Ms. Marr," Leon said. He managed to look boyishly guileless rather than deadly.

"Trina, please," she said with a tremulous smile. Then she looked at Gabe. "They shot at us."

"Yes, they did, and they weren't going for the

tires." Thank God; it had been a miscalculation on their part. "In fact, I'm pretty sure we'll be able to dig a bullet out of one of the seats. It came through the back window but didn't make it to the windshield."

One of Boyd's eyebrows lifted. The bullet would be of limited value unless and until they had a rifle it could be matched with…but Gabe had become grimly determined to bring these scumbags down.

Trina blinked several times as she took in the hard reality that they'd been ambushed by men ready and willing to commit murder to get their hands on a little girl. She finally said, "They were trying to shoot *you*."

"Yep." Although he doubted they'd have quit shooting if they'd seen her.

"They knew Chloe was with us."

That hardly bore comment, since killing Chloe was the idea. Still, frustrated but not surprised that his efforts hadn't been enough, Gabe said, "They did. What's more, they must have seen me taking her inside this morning, otherwise there wouldn't have been time for them to set up."

"And they'd seen which way we went on the highway."

Also not a surprise.

Her gaze stayed fixed on him, as if she'd forgotten the other two men were there. "Do you think they know we're *here*?"

Gabe shook his head. "I've been damn careful not to turn off the highway when any other vehicle was in sight. Twice, I've kept going when I saw another vehicle, even if it was barely a pinprick."

She nodded, having asked him about the first time he'd continued past the ranch road without even having slowed. He'd had to backtrack several miles on both occasions.

"If only the press hadn't found out about me."

"The fire drew a lot of attention," Gabe said gently. "Neighbors were eager to talk about how brave you were, how you saved the life of the little girl you were fostering. The Sadler PD may have trouble keeping secrets, but your name getting out there wasn't their fault."

Trina seemed to sag. "No. Of course not."

Boyd pushed back his chair and rose. "Let me get you something to drink. A beer?"

"Oh…no, thank you." She started to rise, too, but Gabe laid a hand over hers, stopping her. Her startled gaze met his again, and she subsided. "A pop would be great. No, wait. Milk. Milk and cookies, right?"

Boyd smiled, found the right cupboard, and soon brought her a glass of milk. "Beer and cookies work, too." He sat back down and studied the tin. "What kind are those, with the Hershey's Kiss on top?"

"Mint flavored. And those are peanut butter, and I guess the molasses are obvious. I think Gabe ate all the chocolate chip."

He smirked.

He was glad to see her nibbling on a cookie and drinking her milk. An adrenaline crash could do a number on a person. A boost to her blood sugar would help. As soon as the guys left, he'd offer to cook dinner tonight.

"The little girl," Boyd said. "Was she scared?"

Trina nodded. "She sort of…shrank. When bullets started flying, I covered her ears, but…that had to have thrown her back to when her parents and brother were shot, don't you think? She looked glassy-eyed when I put her in front of the movie. I wouldn't have left her, except she did take a bite of her cookie, and I wanted to hear about everything I missed."

"I don't want her to be in the middle of any more violence." The roughness in Gabe's voice had the other three staring at him.

After a minute, Boyd asked matter-of-factly, "What's the plan for tomorrow?"

Gabe's teeth ground together in his effort to give her a chance to make the right decision before he had to force a heated confrontation.

"I can't go to work again." Trina sounded numb. "I shouldn't have insisted."

No, she shouldn't, but… "You had good reason," Gabe said.

"Thank you," she said softly, then jumped up. "I'll start getting dinner on."

He pushed back his chair, too. "Let me do that."

"No, I need to keep busy." She smiled at Boyd and Leon. "You two would be welcome to stay. I'm going to stir-fry, so it won't take long."

Both stood, as well. "Thank you," Boyd said, "but

I'm sure Leon's wife expects him. My housekeeper probably already has dinner on, too."

"Oh. Well." This smile appeared brittle. "Another time."

"Sounds good." Boyd gave a slight nod toward the back door.

Gabe moved toward the door, too. "I'll be right back."

He had no trouble interpreting Trina's expression. She knew they wanted to talk out of her hearing.

Outside, dirt kicking up from every step, Boyd said, "Looked like your truck sustained some damage."

Gabe ground his teeth.

"I know someone over in Salem. I bet I can get him to come over and replace that window."

He sure couldn't replace it locally. If Boyd "knew" this guy and trusted him, he was undoubtedly also retired military. The scrapes and dents from bullets would have to stay for now. He counted his blessings that the idiots hadn't taken out a tire.

"They didn't know about me," he said thoughtfully. "If I didn't have plenty of experience with ambushes, their plan would have worked fine. They got flustered when I didn't stop like a good boy."

"None of them had any serious military training," Leon said.

"No," Gabe agreed, "and I doubt any of them were law enforcement, either. They do roadblocks themselves, would think better under pressure."

"Did you expect them to be cops?" Boyd asked, obviously surprised. "That detective is a nuisance, from the sound of it, but why would he go to these lengths when he could get a subpoena?"

"Because he isn't sure he can? Trina has probably appeared in front of most judges in these parts, her opinion respected. What judge is going to say, 'The woman is trying to protect this kid? Ridiculous! We've got to hurry on this. You go ahead and crack her open.'" He added as an aside, "She heard one of the detectives say that about Chloe. Risvold, especially, is trying hard not to see her as an individual. He wanted to know where Trina had 'stashed' Chloe."

Both the other men were shaking their heads. Leon, he knew, had two kids of his own.

Gabe decided not to say anything about what he'd learned from the Keifs' next-door neighbor last week. The information had been frustrating; the woman had almost certainly seen the killer's car but hadn't paid enough attention to give him much to work with.

It was a sedan, she knew that. Maybe a Lexus? Or a Genesis, or an Acura. It could have been a Cadillac, she'd added. He had later checked online, and could have added to that list. The contours of a number of the big luxury cars were similar, as were grills. "Sort of gray or silver" wasn't real helpful, either. What happened to the days when cars came in real colors?

Having reached Boyd's pickup, Gabe dismissed his frustration and contemplated the out-of-state license plate. "Doesn't look like they so much as tapped your truck."

Boyd laughed. "Not a chance." He sobered. "That gun of yours isn't traceable, is it?"

Gabe pretended indignation. "All those crime sprees I go on, how can I be sure? No. It won't be in any databases."

"Good, we're clear, then. You dig that bullet out and tuck it away." He opened his door. "Let's stay in close touch. Do you have Leon's number, in case I'm unavailable?"

Gabe didn't but entered it in his phone, after which he held out a hand to Leon. "Thanks."

"No problem." The two men shook, and Leon grinned. "A little adrenaline now and again is good for the heart."

Gabe laughed, even though he felt more sick than energized. He didn't go back into the cabin immediately, instead inspecting the damage to his truck.

If Trina had still been sitting up, the bullet that came through the back window might well have hit her in the head. Dead-on. He had a hard time tearing his gaze away from the hole in the front seat headrest.

No, he hadn't gotten any charge out of today's live-round exercise. Protecting Trina and Chloe wasn't a job anymore, or a favor to her brother. It was deeply personal.

Which meant that rage simmered—and he was afraid in a way he hadn't been since he was a boy.

TRINA WAITED UNTIL Chloe was asleep that evening to tell Gabe what little she'd learned today and find out what had happened with the surveillance on Russell Stearns, the fired vice president who'd worked under Michael Keif. Gabe was clearly bothered by Stearns, with good reason. Given how limited opportunities for an executive at his level were in the area, why had he stuck around after he got fired? Had he even interviewed elsewhere? What was he *doing* with his days?

They'd agreed, too, that between patients she should make some calls, find out what she could about Keif, his partner, Pearson, and Stearns.

As usual, they sat at the kitchen table, both with cups of coffee.

She went first. "I called the mother of a boy I worked with for almost a year. Vanessa's job is actually at city hall, in planning, but her husband is an engineer at O.R.E. I was pretty up-front with her, told her about Chloe being too freaked to tell us what she saw, and my worry that's because the 'bad man' is someone she knows."

"And?"

"She was more open than she should have been, really. Vanessa admitted her husband liked Chloe's dad but has problems with Ronald Pearson. Apparently, he pushes to get products out on the market before they've been perfected, and Vanessa's husband, Bob, thinks too many of the company's resources go to maintaining a fleet of trucks. He'd argued to Michael Keif that they should outsource shipping, concentrate on development and manufacturing. Oh, and he'd heard some of the gossip about Russell Stearns but didn't really know him."

She went on to tell him the rest of what she'd gleaned: a female county commissioner whose granddaughter was a current patient had hinted at her dislike of Pearson, calling him "bullish." She didn't think he did his research or had any interest in huge swaths of what the commissioners handled. She'd finished by saying, "He's serving on the board—and I use the word *serving* loosely—to protect his interests. And yes, Michael probably was, too, but he at least did his part. He said he was raising kids here, which made Granger County home." Grief tinged her tone. "I'm sorry he wasn't willing to do another term."

Gabe listened intently, his ability to concentrate without so much as fidgeting out of the ordinary and sometimes a little unsettling.

"None of that is very helpful." She made a face.

"I wouldn't say that. I wonder what 'interests' he's protecting. Is the company polluting? Doesn't seem like manufacturing electronic components would lead to that kind of problem, but you never know. Or is he concerned O.R.E. might be expected to come through for additional traffic mitigation? Taxes? They're mostly state and federal." He seemed to shake himself. "Stearns played a round of golf this morning. I took some photos so I can try to identify the others in the foursome. He had lunch with a woman—" Gabe named the fanciest restaurant in Sadler "—escorted her to her car and then followed her out to O.R.E. She went into the executive offices on her own, never glanced back. Couldn't tell if she was pretending she didn't know him, or whether she hadn't realized he was behind her. He gave her a couple of minutes, then went into the office building, too, stayed for about an hour, strolled out looking unconcerned."

"They're really going to hire him back."

"Probably. But I wonder about the woman. I haven't had a chance to identify her yet, either. Is he seeing her because he thinks she can help his cause?"

"Hmm. I bet Vanessa could find out—"

"You don't have your phone, remember?"

She mumbled a swear word. Except for when she'd been at work, she hadn't had her phone for nearly two weeks, so why did the reminder make her feel so isolated now? So she'd lost some independence. It was temporary, and Joseph would probably be making the same decisions Gabe was.

Suck it up, she told herself.

"Are you going to call Detective Risvold tomorrow?" she asked. Gabe had already asked if they needed any groceries, so she knew he was planning a trip to Bend in the morning.

"I don't like it that Risvold was the one who talked to the Keifs' neighbor and apparently didn't ask if she'd been home, and if so, taken a look in the direction of their house around about the time of the murders. That feels off."

It felt "off" to her, too, but then she'd despised Risvold almost from their first meeting. That didn't mean he'd gone to the dark side.

"His style is brisk," she pointed out. "He might have assumed she'd be eager to tell him if she'd seen anything."

Gabe grimaced. "Yeah, okay. I'll call him."

Trina nodded, realizing that, for the first time in her life, she couldn't begin to identify everything she felt. Terror was easy—all she had to do was remember the fire—or, nice addition, lying nose down on the rubber mat on the floor behind Gabe's seat while the truck rocked violently, the back window dissolved and bullets pinged on metal. Intense gratitude was in the mix, as was resentment because she was having to depend so utterly on another person, when she'd taken care of herself for a long time.

But now, looking across the table at his hard face and the blue eyes that never wavered from her, she untangled another thread of her emotions. Trust. She didn't believe Gabe Decker would ever let her down.

And that made her wonder if what he'd said the one night—*You have to know I'm feeling things for you*—didn't have a lot deeper meaning than she'd read into it. It wasn't as if she'd expected him to tell her he was madly in love with her, not so soon. That awkward admission might have been his equivalent of passionate declaration.

Which meant maybe she ought to trust him in *every* way.

She took a deep breath, saw a flicker in his eyes and nerved herself to ask, "Will you kiss me?"

Chapter Nine

Trina had a bad feeling Gabe would think she was a flake. Yes, no, yes, no. Bungee cord bounces in the messages she had been sending.

But he didn't even hesitate. He exploded into motion, his chair clattering back, and he reached her in two strides. She expected to be grabbed, for him to take powerful, sensual control immediately.

Instead, he cupped her face in his broad palms and bent his head slowly. His gentle kiss came as a surprise. His mouth brushed hers. He nibbled a little. His tongue stroked the seam of her lips.

Through the fog in her head, Trina realized he was giving her time. Waiting for an answer.

What do you really want? Why did you change your mind?

She'd changed it because she didn't want to miss something amazing out of fear.

She pushed herself up on tiptoe, wrapped her arms around his neck and nipped his lower lip sharply.

A groan rumbled out of his chest, and yes, he took

charge, because that's who he was. Didn't mean she couldn't kiss him back with everything in her. One of his hands gripped her hip while the other wrapped the back of her head so he could angle her to find the best fit.

And the fit was amazing. Perfect. His neck was thick and strong, his entire body powerful. That body was so close she could feel the vibration of his heartbeat. When he breathed, her nipples tightened.

The kiss went on and on, until the rest of the world might as well not have existed. He was everything. Trina heard odd sounds, and distantly knew they came from her. She wanted to climb his body, and was practically *en pointe* in her effort to get higher. She must have raised one of her legs, because he made a guttural sound, shifted so that he could grip both of her thighs and lifted her. She squeaked, wrapped her legs around his waist and held on.

Somehow he walked and kissed her at the same time. And they said men didn't multitask as well as women. Here was an exception. The way she felt, Trina wasn't sure she'd have cared if he *had* banged her into a wall or the staircase banister, but that never happened. At the foot of the stairs, though, he stopped. When his mouth left hers, she rubbed her cheek against his rough jaw, then did some experimental nibbling.

"Trina." That deep, dark voice felt as good as his hands on her.

She licked his neck, tasting soap and salt.

"Trina." This time he shook her.

Dazed, she tipped her head back to see a look of pure desperation on his face.

"Do you want this?"

Want this? She was on fire. No, bad analogy. Fire *hurt*. This was…hunger. An aching kind of pleasure. She tried to rub herself against him.

"To hell with it," he muttered, and started up the stairs. Once he stopped to kiss her, swore when they swayed and wrenched his mouth away. Reaching the top, he strode down the hall.

Trina felt a momentary jolt at the sight of the guest room door, standing open the requisite four inches. What if Chloe saw…? But Trina didn't hear anything from within. Or without. Gabe had the ability to walk silently, even carrying her. He got her through his bedroom doorway without a single bump. He must have nudged the door with his booted foot, because it closed quietly behind them.

Enough light from the hall reached into his bedroom for her to be able to see fierce need on his face, so far from his usual, carefully assumed lack of expression that her meltdown accelerated.

Beside the bed, he lowered her slowly to her feet. After sliding down his body, she wasn't so sure she could stand, but she managed. Lucky, because he used the opportunity to first rip the bedcoverings back and then strip her with astonishing speed.

"You, too," she whispered, and he paused long

enough to let her pull his shirt over his head, baring that broad, muscular chest.

He knelt to take off her shoes and pull her jeans off. Trina braced herself by resting her hands on his shoulders. Except that wasn't enough. She kneaded, felt the ripples of reaction quiver through his strong body. And then he surged up, laid her back on the bed and planted a knee between her thighs.

He reached out a long arm and flicked on the bedside lamp. Trina blinked in the sudden light, not sure she liked being so exposed…except the look in his eyes was reverential.

"You're as beautiful as I thought you'd be," he murmured in the voice that reminded her of her first impression: the rumbling purr of a big cat.

"You are, too." She flattened her hands on his chest, then moved them in circles. The dark hair beneath her palms was surprisingly soft. He jerked when she found his small nipples. Swore when her hands stroked downward, following the line of hair to the waistband of his jeans.

When she lifted a hand to cover the hard ridge beneath the fly, he straightened away from her. "Damn. Give me a minute."

He had to sit on the side of the bed to remove his boots. She happily explored the contours of muscle on his back, flexing with his every movement. Socks went flying. He stood and shed jeans and shorts. And then, finally, he came down on top of her and went for her mouth again.

They discovered each other's tastes and textures. He sucked on her breasts until her hips rose and fell. The frustration of being able to feel him between her thighs drove her crazy.

Trina moaned and dug her fingernails into his sides. "Now. Please, now."

He swore some more, and for the first time displayed clumsiness as he fumbled for the drawer of his bedside stand and found some packets. He tore one with his teeth, covered himself and without an instant of hesitation, pressed into her.

She pushed herself up to meet him. Gabe muttered something under his breath, covered her mouth with his again and set a hard, fast rhythm that was exactly what she needed.

Not until she imploded and cried out did he let himself go.

IN THE AFTERMATH, Gabe didn't want to move. Ever again. But damn, he must be crushing her. Reluctantly, he rolled, taking her with him. She ended up with her head on his chest, her hand splayed over his heart and one leg draped over his.

Holy hell, he thought dazedly. He liked sex, missed it during intervals when it wasn't possible. But what he and Trina had just done? The equivalent of an explosion versus him stubbing his toe.

Of course, he knew why that was. He'd never before felt more than attraction and mild liking for a woman he took to bed. Trina was different. So many unfamiliar emotions churned in his chest, he envisioned those pictures he'd seen of hurricanes taken from the space station. The relentless force spinning, unstoppable by human hands. The layers upon layers that made up the monstrous power unleashed by nature. The still, quiet eye at the center.

He clenched his teeth together. Man, what was getting into him? This was ridiculous. Okay, he felt more for her than he'd ever let himself feel for any woman. After struggling to come up with a label for one component, he finally did. Tenderness. That was something he'd lived his entire life without.

The respect...that was what he had for his teammates. Men who had proved themselves, who had his unshakable trust.

He lifted his head from the mattress so he could see her face, but he discovered hair that looked more than ever like melted caramel blocked his view.

Trina Marr, he thought, suddenly uneasy, could be trusted. She'd committed herself to Chloe, and would do anything for her. She wasn't the kid's mother, but she acted as if she was.

Except he, of all people, knew mothers weren't always trustworthy.

With no inner debate at all, he realized there wasn't any chance this woman had that flaw.

In fact, she was unnervingly like her brother in some respects. The steady gaze that saw deeper than he liked. The stubbornness, the courage, the determination that kept her going no matter what flew her way.

Damn. He was scaring himself. This thing with her couldn't go anywhere. He'd be back at Fort Benning in no time, training for the next operation in some hellhole. She'd…fade in his memory. She had to, or he'd be in deep trouble.

She stirred, puffed out a breath that fluttered her hair and reached up to push it away from her face. "Wow," she mumbled.

A smile tugged at his mouth. He liked that he'd left her befuddled. It almost made up for his confusion.

He let his hand wander now, exploring the long, taut line of her back and the delicate string of vertebrae. All of her bones felt fine to him, almost fragile compared to his.

Hard not to remember how easily his had shattered. Hers…no. He wouldn't let anyone hurt her.

"How do you stay in such good shape?" Probably not the most romantic thing to have said, but he was curious.

Her nose scrunched up. "Gym. Self-torture."

He laughed. "You could find a sport you enjoy, you know."

"Oh, I have. I do. I love riding, and swimming is okay, but the most effective is the elliptical and the treadmill. I'd probably run outside, but around here it's either too hot or too miserably cold. Not much in between."

"Ever tried racquetball?"

"I don't like things flying at me."

They had something in common; Gabe definitely didn't like bullets flying at him.

He chuckled, rubbed his face against her head to feel the sleek silk of her hair and decided not to ruin a good moment by worrying. He could enjoy, couldn't he?

Except she sighed, a puff of air he felt on his chest, and said, "I should go back to my bed."

Gabe quit breathing, just held himself still. "Why?"

"Chloe will be scared if she wakes up to find herself alone."

"She's used to being alone in bed for a couple of hours before you join her." What was he arguing for? Her to stay the night? To keep this casual, it would be better if she didn't.

Trina was quiet for a minute. "Can I ask you something?"

Immediately wary, he said, "Is this a 'get in my head' question?"

"Well, kind of. No, more me wanting to know you."

Because of Joseph, he knew quite a bit about her childhood. The loving parents, the tight family. His past was a blank to her.

"You can ask," he said after a minute.

"Do you have family? People you stay in touch with, who worry about you?"

He didn't talk about this. But… Trina was different.

Throat tight, he said, "No."

"I guess I knew that." She sounded sad.

Was he going to do this? "Never even knew who my father was," he said hoarsely. "My mother was an addict. She died when I was five. I barely remember her."

"I'm so sorry." She turned her head enough to press a kiss to his chest. "I don't suppose you were adopted."

"No." He hesitated. "A rancher took me on as a foster kid when I was fourteen. I stayed until I graduated from high school. He was a quiet guy. I thought he needed some extra labor. But…"

"But?" she prodded, when he didn't finish.

"He died when I was in my early twenties. Left me the ranch." Gabe stared up at the rafters. "It wasn't a huge place, but it had a year-round creek running through it. Two neighboring ranchers bid each other up, and I came out of it with enough money to let me pay for half of this place, when the chance came."

"You didn't expect anything from your foster father."

It wasn't a question; she knew. But he shook his head anyway. "No. I wish I'd known—" His throat seized up.

"That he loved you?"

Had he? Gabe still didn't know.

He felt something warm and…wet? She wasn't crying, was she? He touched her face to find she was.

"I haven't been a kid for a long time, Trina."

"But you intend to stay alone, don't you?"

A spasm seemed to close his throat completely, when he should be saying yes. Reminding her that this was recreational sex. But somehow he couldn't speak at all. Which was fortunate, because for the first time in his life, he wasn't sure what he'd have said. What he thought was, *That's what I always figured.*

Past tense.

He was stunned to realize that the unexpected, unwelcome feelings he had for this woman had him in a tighter grip than he'd imagined. He wanted her to worry about him. He wanted to know she was waiting at home for him. And *this* felt like home: him, her, the ranch, his cabin...and Chloe.

In a panic, he stayed silent. Instead, he rolled on his side and kissed her, until neither of them could think about past or future. Only now.

TRINA WAS SOUND ASLEEP and really wanted to stay that way, but the mattress bobbed like a wave-tossed boat. She groaned, pried open her eyelids and found Chloe jumping on the bed about a foot from her.

"Go 'way," she mumbled.

"Uh-*uh*. Gabe says to tell you it's breakfast time."

Trina whimpered and buried her face. Chloe kept bouncing.

Well, at least she wasn't mute and sad. Why wasn't she, given yesterday's terrifying events?

Probably, Trina realized, because she hadn't really known what was happening. Chloe had to have heard the gunshots, though. Was there any chance they hadn't triggered panic because whoever killed her family had used a silencer?

Sad to say, Trina realized, she was definitely awake. "Okay, okay."

Once Chloe was satisfied that Trina was really getting up, she scampered away. A shower mostly finished the job. When she got out, though, she saw herself in the foggy mirror and froze. Grabbing the hand towel, she swiped at the glass and kept staring. There were an awful lot of…not bruises, but red spots. Probably from Gabe's stubble, she thought in chagrin. At the time, it had felt good.

So good, in fact, that her whole body tingled as she remembered their lovemaking.

Even the weight of his silence after her question didn't squelch the tingles.

Trust, she reminded herself. He had talked to her. And he hadn't said, *Yeah, I'm a loner*. His silence gave her hope she could change his mind.

And wasn't that typical female idiocy, believing she could change a man? But that wasn't it; she liked him, could even love him, exactly the way he was. If only…

She made a horrible face at herself in the mirror and got dressed.

When she went downstairs, Gabe gave her a hard, searching look that she returned with a feeble smile. Creases formed on his forehead.

She ate the pancakes he put in front of her, and produced a short grocery list for him when he reminded her that he was going shopping. Since he'd shopped Saturday, she didn't need anything, but it wouldn't hurt to have him pick up some fresh veggies, not to mention milk. They were going through an awful lot of it.

Chloe watched them. "You don't hafta work?"

Trina did a little better with this smile. "Nope. I'm taking a vacation."

The little girl brightened. "Can I ride Mack today?"

"Yep," Gabe promised. "Later. I have to do errands this morning."

"We could ride and then you could do errands," Chloe said slyly.

He laughed, came around the breakfast bar to swing her in the air. Depositing her back on the stool, he said, "Good try, but no."

"Well, poop."

He only laughed again, kissed Trina on the cheek and left, after extracting a renewed promise that they stay inside and not answer the door. Fingertips pressed to the exact spot on her cheek that he'd kissed, she watched as his truck passed the cabin, then turned toward the ranch proper rather than the highway.

He was on his way to borrow yet another pickup truck from a ranch hand, and presumably took along another of those burner phones he'd bought as if every man kept a selection on hand.

Because while he did intend to grocery-shop, he also planned to call Risvold.

Trina's skin felt too tight the whole time he was gone. What if someone came to the door? What would Detective Risvold say after Gabe told him about the ambush?

Would Gabe want her to spend most of the night in his bed again?

At six minutes past eleven o'clock, Trina saw the borrowed truck pass out on the ranch road. Not that she was watching or anything. But thank goodness, he'd only been gone two hours.

A few minutes later, he returned in his truck. She hovered in the kitchen, waiting for him. He walked in the back door laden with bags from a grocery store and Target, and glanced around. "Where's Chloe?"

"Living room. She loves those puzzles you bought."

His smile formed lines in his cheeks. "I noticed." He hefted one of the bags. "Four more."

After he plopped them down on the counter, Trina delved into the bag and saw, in delight, that his choices were perfect. The one on top was a unicorn. But, bless his heart, he'd also bought a puzzle with pirates, one with an animal alphabet and a barnyard puzzle.

"Thought we'd go for the dinosaur puzzle next time, and maybe the big trucks."

How could he possibly believe he shouldn't have a family, that he wouldn't make a wonderful father?

After thanking him, she asked, "Did you reach Detective Risvold?"

Gabe went to the refrigerator and grabbed a bottle of water before he pulled out a stool and half sat, one foot braced on the floor. "No, I talked to Detective Deperro instead. Risvold was out. Deperro seemed a little less…aggressive."

"I had the same impression. Did you tell him about the ambush?"

A glint in Gabe's eyes, he said, "I didn't share every detail, but yes. I said two vehicles, four men, tried a pincer move on us. They barricaded the highway, shot at us. I'd swear he was genuinely stunned, although he could have been playing me."

"Did you give him the license plate number?"

They'd talked about this before he left this morning. He had a friend who was a cop in Portland, and Gabe had intended to ask him to run the number.

Gabe's forehead furrowed, but he said, "I'm not sure I would have if it had been Risvold, but…yeah. Doesn't mean I won't tap my friend, too. We can call this a test. In fact, I'll call Alan this morning."

Trina told him her speculation that Chloe hadn't actually heard gunshots when her parents and brothers were killed.

"Not a silencer, a suppressor," Gabe said absently. "That's a good thought, although I'm not sure knowing one way or the other helps us identify the killer."

"Most normal people wouldn't have one. In fact, aren't they illegal or something?"

"Not in Oregon, although theoretically you have to get BATF approval to buy one." He paused, interpreted her expression accurately. "Bureau of Alcohol, Tobacco and Firearms."

"Oh." She frowned. "Do you have a permit for that handgun?"

"Don't need one in this state. For concealed carry, you do." His lips twitched. "I haven't bothered yet. I'm not spending that much time here, and until I met you, I didn't have any need to carry a weapon at all."

"Oh. I'm sorry."

"Don't be," he said brusquely. "Truth is, I was feeling pretty damn useless until you came along."

Trina blinked at that, and wasn't surprised when he turned his back to put groceries away. The conversation was over.

Her temper spiked. No, it wasn't. "What did Detective Deperro *say*?"

Gabe dumped several plastic bags with vegetables into the refrigerator and closed it before facing her again. "He wanted to know who I am. Swore he wasn't trying to track down you and Chloe."

She snorted, sounding an awful lot like his horse.

"He didn't say much, but his frustration came through loud and clear. I didn't get the feeling he's happy with how the investigation is going. Or not going. I asked about the random guy wandering through the neighborhood. He told me straight-out that they'd never taken that seriously."

"Then why did Risvold try to feed that crap to me?" she exclaimed.

"Because he didn't like the idea of you expecting information to go two ways?" Gabe suggested. He leaned against the counter and crossed his booted feet at the ankles. "I'm damn sure he didn't want you to know if they were looking at Pearson or anyone else close to the family."

"I've worked with children involved in a criminal investigation twice before. That detective trusted me enough to be frank. Of course, being a woman, she probably doesn't have the same territorial issues."

Gabe grinned, startling her into instant, intense awareness of him lounging there not three feet from her. Even with that big body ostensibly relaxed, she didn't make the mistake of believing she could catch him off guard. Nope, she'd seen a demonstration of how lightning fast his reflexes were.

"You might be right," he said, the smile lingering on his mouth. For a moment, they just looked at each other. Then he pushed himself away from the cabinet. "Hey. Come here."

She sneaked a peek toward the living room. "I should check on—"

"Can you hear her?"

"Hear?" She concentrated. He was right—Chloe was singing softly to herself. Trina smiled and stepped forward into his arms, which folded around her. Splaying her fingers on his chest, she said, "She'll be in here any minute demanding to ride your horsie, because you said 'later' and it *is* later."

He laughed, and nuzzled her cheek. "Sure, but she isn't here yet. And why waste an opportunity?"

He captured her mouth and made good use of their time.

Chapter Ten

Gabe decided to call his friend Portland police detective Alan Cullen before he did a single other thing. Fortunately, Alan returned Gabe's call within ten minutes.

"You're the last person I expected to hear from," he said. "I thought you were still in rehab at Fort Benning."

Sitting out on the front porch in an Adirondack chair, Gabe grimaced. Alan had been a good enough friend, he should have gotten in touch sometime in the last year. Loner that he was, he'd resisted even depending on Boyd. "I've been at the ranch for a couple of months. The damn rehab has dragged on."

"Then what's with the license plate number?"

Gabe gave him a synopsis of events, and even that took a few minutes. Voice changing as he shifted into cop-mode, Alan asked a few questions.

"Damn," he said at last. "Joseph Marr's sister. Lucky you were available. Although I suppose Joseph could have called Boyd instead."

Feeling instant resistance, even repugnance, Gabe ground his teeth before forcing himself to say, "I guess so." He'd seen the way Boyd looked at Trina the first time he and she had met. Hell. What if she and Boyd—

He shook off the possibility because it made him so angry.

"Okay, what's the license plate number?" Alan asked.

Gabe read it off.

"I can run it right—" The silence didn't last long. "Huh."

"What's that mean?"

"It's tagged. Belongs on a charcoal gray Audi RS7. Was it fast?"

"Oh, yeah."

"Six hundred and five horsepower engine." The remark was absent; it wasn't what Alan was really thinking about. "Registered owner is a guy named Craig Jarvis. He's ostensibly an importer, but the DEA has their suspicions about him."

Drug Enforcement Administration? Gabe felt as if a critical puzzle piece had been inserted. Dark corners were suddenly bathed in harsh white light.

"Does he live on this side of the mountains?" he asked.

"Yes, Bend." Alan paused. "You know central Oregon has become a hotbed of drug trafficking, don't you? Lots of small airfields, rural sheriffs' departments that don't have the manpower to monitor odd comings and goings. There are several drug task forces over there, although—" he paused "—it doesn't look like your county is included. Attention has focused on the major highways—I-5, of course, but also Interstate 84 and highways 97 and 20. You're not on any of those, but a county with so little population might be ideal for bringing drugs in from Mexico and Central America. Distribution could be tricky, though."

"I have a good idea how the drugs are getting distributed," Gabe said tightly. He told Alan what he was thinking, and how drug trafficking might well have led to the murders.

"You need to contact the Oregon HIDTA Investigative Support Center. They coordinate information for federal, state and local law enforcement within their counties."

"Granger County is outside their jurisdiction."

"You think they won't jump on this?"

"Maybe." Sometime during this conversation, he'd risen to his feet, too tense now to sit. He stood at the porch railing, looking at the dry forest surrounding his cabin. "I need to think about this. Tell me you don't have any obligation to contact anyone."

There was a short silence. "What's your hesitation?"

"First, why hasn't Sadler PD brought in some help?"

"You so sure they haven't?" Alan asked.

"Not positive," Gabe admitted with reluctance. "I

did pass on the same license plate tag to one of the detectives. But damn it, there hasn't been so much as a hint that they're considering a drug trafficking angle. Even I'd begun to feel uneasy when several people mentioned the conflict at Open Range Electronics over whether they ought to maintain their own trucks versus shipping through other companies."

"What's your real problem?" That was like Alan— get to the point.

"Trina and Chloe," Gabe said without hesitation. "If either of us talks to any law enforcement agency, they're going to get right back to the investigators in Sadler. With my name. It would mean moving Trina and the girl, at the very least. I'm not letting them out of my sight. So then all three of us would be AWOL and hunted, and I'll tell you, Alan, I think Sadler PD has a leak."

"It wouldn't be a shock if a major trafficking organization had bought themselves a cop or two," his friend conceded. "But…hell. How are you going to handle it on your own?"

"Don't know yet. No, I realize we'll have to trust someone, sooner or later, but right now all I have is speculation. If those two detectives aren't wondering the same thing you and I are, then they're even more incompetent than I believed."

"I'll give you that." Alan gusted a sigh. "This is your call, not mine. But if I can do anything, I will, even if it's bailing you out of jail."

Gabe's grunt was almost a laugh. "What are friends for?"

"Keep me informed."

They left it at that. Gabe stayed where he was for a long while, even though Chloe must be bouncing off the walls with impatience for the promised horse-back ride.

What if Michael Keif had somehow discovered that his company trucks were being used to trans-port illegal drugs? Drugs that might even be packed in O.R.E.-labeled boxes? Everything he'd worked for would be at risk of going down if even one truck was searched and the drugs were found. The feds would have descended like army airborne troops on a known terrorist hideout.

Pearson was the executive whose responsibilities included the trucking fleet. He was also the one who resisted suggestions that it was too expensive to main-tain compared to alternatives.

Gabe also had to consider the possibility that someone lower on the org chart had set up a deal with traffickers. It didn't have to be Pearson.

Either way, Russell Stearns could have learned what was going on, and wanted a slice of the pie. He might have felt confident that if Keif were out of the picture, he'd be asked to take his place—and would then be in a position to enrich himself by abetting, or at least turning a blind eye to, any and all illegal activities, for a payoff.

Damn, Gabe wished he trusted either of the two

detectives. He'd had a better feeling about Deperro…
but not enough to risk giving away Trina and Chloe's
whereabouts.

Maybe Boyd knew of someone well-placed whom
he trusted. Worth asking. Otherwise… Gabe gave his
head a hard shake, trying to stir thoughts, worries,
ideas, in hopes they'd resettle in a new arrangement.

They didn't.

His next step…

The front door opened behind him and a small
voice said, "Can't we ride *now*?"

He gave a rueful smile. Keeping a promise came
next.

TRINA ENJOYED TODAY'S RIDE even more than she had
the other day. Gabe chose a different route, one that
allowed them to ride side by side much of the time.
They passed through several gates and pastures, cows
and calves watching them from a distance. Apparently, he'd decided that since neither had been sore
from the last ride, they were up to a longer one today.

They hadn't had a chance for him to tell her about
the conversation with his cop friend. She'd worried
when he first came back into the cabin with Chloe,
though. The lines scored on his forehead looked per-
manent, and she'd swear the grooves in his cheeks
hadn't been that deep before. But he had gradually
relaxed after saddling the horses, lifting Chloe up
and then swinging up behind her.

He proved willing to talk about the ranch, and even

a little bit about his teenage years in Texas. "Hooked me on the life," he admitted. "I'd hate being trapped indoors every day, stuck behind a desk."

Trina learned this was an enormous operation, and Boyd and Gabe fully intended to expand it. Literally, since they were keeping an eye out for any land bordering theirs to go on the market, and also because both men were interested in breeding and training horses on a larger scale than they were currently doing.

"Boyd's waiting for you to retire?" she asked.

"Yeah." Gabe paused, perturbation momentarily reversing the relaxation she'd seen on his face. "No hurry, though."

This wasn't a man who'd let a mere injury stop him, she realized anew. That grim determination was to her benefit right now, hers and Chloe's, but it also meant he wouldn't let a hookup with some woman prevent him from returning to what really mattered to him.

Her trust that he might actually feel more for her than he wanted to admit dissipated into near nothingness.

"*I* want to be a horsie rancher," Chloe announced, proving she'd been listening. "'Cept, I've never seen a baby horse."

"They're called foals," he said, with a gentleness that always made Trina's heart feel as if it were developing fissures. "And since they're usually born in the spring, we have some right now. We can go look at the mares and foals tomorrow, if you want."

Planning happy activities laid a veneer over the reality that they were hiding out, waiting for... Trina hardly knew anymore. Chloe to tell them who had killed her daddy? Would they really be safe once that happened?

She realized they'd made a gradual circle and were nearing Gabe's cabin and barns again. Probably just as well; her thighs were starting to ache.

Today, Gabe let her unsaddle her borrowed mount and turn him out in the paddock. Still holding the bridle, Trina heard a distant buzz. Puzzled, she swiveled in place, trying to identify the source of the sound. It was a motor of some kind. An ATV, maybe? She knew that ranchers did sometimes use them in place of horses to herd cattle.

"Into the barn," Gabe said suddenly. *"Now."*

The sound was increasing in intensity and volume. Maybe it was the crack of his voice, maybe some subliminal fear, but she scooped up Chloe and ran. Gabe was right behind. In seconds, they reached the shadowy interior of the barn that had several stalls, hay storage above and a tack room.

He pulled the sliding door almost closed, leaving a three-inch gap to admit sunlight and give him a view out.

"It's a helicopter," Trina whispered, as if they might be overheard.

"It is." He stood where he could see out, his face

set, his body still but the furthest thing from relaxed. This was the soldier, coiled to take action.

An unarmed soldier, she realized in sudden alarm. Trina clutched Chloe tight.

Gabe started to swear, not quite under his breath, but then he glanced at Chloe and clamped his mouth shut.

The sound of the whirling rotors became deafening. Chloe cried out and clapped her hands over her ears. Trina held her breath, as if she were a small animal caught in the open when the shadow of a falcon swept over her.

Gabe never moved, but she swore the band of light dimmed. Was the helicopter hovering right overhead? Or landing? Images from war movies flickered in her head. No wonder that sound had seemed so ominous.

And then the roar began to recede. Trina sagged, stepping back to allow herself to lean against the rough board wall of the tack room.

"Where's it going?" Her voice was too loud.

"The ranch center." He sounded remarkably normal. "Let's dash for the cabin."

Trina smiled for Chloe's benefit. "Okeydoke. That was noisy, wasn't it?"

Trembling, Chloe asked, "What was that?"

Halfway across the open ground, Gabe reached for Chloe and lifted her into his own arms. "It was a helicopter passing overhead. Have you ever seen one?"

Puckers appeared in the high, curved forehead. "I think so," she said uncertainly. "It landed on top of the hospital. Daddy—" her voice hitched "—said sometimes sick people ride in one 'stead of an ambulance."

"That's right." Gabe had the back door open and ushered Trina in. She heard the dead bolt *snick* behind them. "Helicopters are faster than ambulances. They fly right over stop signs and red lights."

Chloe decided then and there that she needed the bathroom. Trina hurried her to the one on this floor, then settled her with one of her new puzzles, promising lunch in a few minutes.

Just as she returned to the kitchen, Gabe's phone rang.

"Oh, yeah," he said, seconds into the call. "Did you get a look at it?"

Boyd, she realized. Unfortunately, Gabe's end of the conversation wasn't very illuminating.

He concluded the call and dropped the phone on the counter. Standing a few feet from her, he said, "The helicopter stampeded some cattle and horses. Boyd is seriously pissed. He grabbed binoculars but insists there were no visible markings. The windshield was tinted. Had to be private. I've seen the sheriff's department search and rescue helicopter. It's bigger than this one, white with green stripes and the department logo. Medic helicopters are conspicuously marked, too. I've sure never seen one locally that was black."

"Black seems sort of…" Trina searched for a word. "Covert?"

"Well, yes."

"It definitely was. All aircraft are required to have what's called an 'N' number painted in a conspicuous place. There are rules about how tall the letters and numbers have to be. Boyd thinks the number must have been taped or painted over."

She was almost surprised to see that her hand was steady as she chopped hard-boiled eggs in preparation for making egg salad sandwiches. "So, does that mean they know we're here?" *They* were more frightening because they remained faceless, their numbers unknown. Bad enough when she'd thought there was a killer, singular.

Gabe touched her, his knuckles light on her cheek. She let herself lean into the touch, just for a minute.

"No," he said huskily. "Boyd made some calls. We know for sure the damn thing flew over several other ranches out here, at least. Could have been a dozen or more. Having it go over that low scared the crap out of a lot of cattle and horses. The sheriff's department and the FAA are getting some irate phone calls." He smiled slightly. "Boyd is joining them."

"Good!"

"Won't do any good, of course, when nobody can identify the damn thing. Whoever was flying it had to know there'd be an uproar. My guess is the helicopter will be grounded for a while."

"I wonder if O.R.E. has one for the executives."

"That's an excellent question." Gabe leaned against

the cabinet. "I'll do some research. If they do, it has to be registered."

"This is my fault." She looked toward the kitchen window but was aware of it only as a bright rectangle. She'd already been brooding about this but had comforted herself that the men would have no way of narrowing their search. She'd been wrong. If Gabe had left his truck outside today, or had been returning from one of his expeditions, they'd have been located. "They know Chloe and I are hiding out near here because I insisted on going to work. It was so stupid." Shaking her head, she rinsed her hands, then stood with them dripping into the sink. She hated having to see his expression but finally turned her head. "You didn't have a gun out there. If they'd landed…"

His eyes were warm, nothing like she'd expected. Gripping her shoulders, he said, "Okay, one thing at a time. First, I've been keeping a rifle in the barn. If that damn thing had looked like it was settling on the ground, I'd have had the rifle in my hands. I didn't want to scare Chloe."

"Oh. Okay."

He drew her toward him, not seeming to care that the hands she flattened on his chest were still wet. She was vaguely surprised they didn't steam, given his body heat.

"Second," he said sternly, "yeah, they have a geographic fix on us because you and I were going back and forth to town. But we were doing that for good reason. Two reasons. You do good working with those kids, Trina. And something I didn't tell you. Risvold claimed if you didn't show up for work, he'd assume you'd skipped the area. He made some threats. No matter what, if I hadn't agreed that the risk was justified, I'd have said no."

Guilt morphed into annoyance, even though she should be glad he was accepting responsibility, too. "So I had no real say?"

"You had a say. My decision would have been final."

"Does the word *arrogant* ring any bells?"

He smiled slightly.

She was being absurd. This wasn't a battle of the sexes. It was survival.

"Will you show me where you keep that rifle?" she said steadily, stepping back. "In case…"

"Yes." Gabe frowned. "Damn, I should have already done that. Have you ever handled a gun?"

"Are you kidding? Joseph has done his best to prepare me for any of life's eventualities. Riots, earthquakes, muggers, zombies, you name it, I'm ready." But not a house fire, she thought. Not arson. And he hadn't covered the unit on evasive driving.

Leaning a hip against the cabinet, Gabe laughed, as she'd intended. "I don't suppose you target-practice?"

She wrinkled her nose. "I haven't in a while. Brother dear would disapprove if he knew how lax I've been. But I do know what I'm doing with a hunting rifle or a handgun."

"Good." Leaning forward, he brushed his lips over

hers, kissed her forehead and released her. "I hear the munchkin coming."

"Oh! I need to get these sandwiches made."

Quietly, he said, "I'll show you while she's napping."

Trina became aware of the tension between her shoulder blades and creeping up her neck. They wouldn't be making passionate love during Chloe's nap time, they'd be inspecting available armaments.

Because this was war, wasn't it?

GABE TOLD TRINA the combination to the gun safe, then had her handle the smallest handgun he owned, the one best suited to a woman, as well as a black hunting rifle. She loaded magazines and unloaded them. He'd have liked to have her do some shooting, but they couldn't afford for anyone to hear the barrage of gunfire, so he settled for satisfying himself that she appeared competent with a weapon in her hand.

Then, unhappy, he vowed to do his damnedest to be here 24/7 to protect her and Chloe. For all he knew, Trina had the skills of a sharpshooter, but he had a lot of trouble imagining her pinning a man in her sights and pulling the trigger. She was a woman of warmth and compassion, one who'd chosen to work with traumatized children. He suspected she would be able to pull that trigger if she believed it was the only way to save the little girl she so obviously loved. And then she'd have to live with what she'd done.

Gabe had killed often enough, he ought to be utterly hardened to the necessity and the aftermath. In one way, he was. He'd learned to compartmentalize, a term one of those damn therapists at the army hospital liked to throw around. It wasn't a bad description, he'd decided. For the most part, he put those memories in a drawer rarely opened. He'd never discussed it with any of his friends and teammates, but he suspected they did the same, whatever imagery they used.

That didn't mean he didn't dream, wasn't blindsided on occasion by a memory of the face of a man just before he died—or *as* he died, which was worse. His drawer didn't seem to have a secure lock holding it closed.

If Trina had to shoot to kill, she'd be haunted by what she'd done for the rest of her life. She wasn't him. She saw the humanity in everyone, believed in the possibility of goodness.

The minute the gun safe was securely locked, he left her. He didn't let himself look back, even though he knew she watched him go. He could work out and still be close by if someone showed up. Slacking off the way he had been wasn't acceptable. Nothing had changed. He had a goal.

Once in the makeshift gym in the other half of the outbuilding where he parked his truck, Gabe warmed up, then did some squats and lunges while holding weights. He welcomed the burn of straining muscles and ignored the deeper, more ominous pain in his pelvis and thigh. He added ten pounds to the barbell, lay back on his weight bench and began a methodical series of presses, sweat stinging his eyes and soaking his shirt.

Finally, he let the barbell crash onto its stand and swore, long and viciously. His ability to focus had always been unshakable. So why couldn't he get Trina out of his head?

Chapter Eleven

Gabe had trouble looking away from Trina during dinner, even though he could tell he was making her uncomfortable. After his earlier brooding, he tried to understand his physical fascination with her. He studied every changing flicker of expression on her face, the tiny dimple that formed to the right of her mouth when she tried to suppress a smile, the rich depths of her eyes, the way light reflected off her hair. He liked that her ears stuck out a little bit, that her upper lip had a deep dip in the center.

Yeah, he'd gotten in over his head, all right.

He'd known beautiful, leggy, curvy women before, which meant that calling his obsession with Trina physical might not be right. It was definitely part of it, though. Man, he hoped she planned to join him in his bed tonight.

The way she chattered with Chloe, he wondered if she was feeling shy with him. Would he need to ask? Beg? His chest felt tight, his belly in a knot. The vegetarian chili she'd made was great, but he ate mechanically, his appetite not really there.

He hadn't lived with a woman and child since he was a kid himself. The proximity with Trina and yeah, the little girl, too, was doing a number on him. If anything, he disliked leaving them alone even more now, after the helicopter had damn near skimmed the peak of the cabin roof. If they'd been outside while he ran errands, he could have come home to find them gone. Just like that.

Or dead. One of those sons of bitches in the helicopter could have showered them with bullets, left them sprawled in the dirt.

Gabe suddenly realized the other two were staring at him, as if waiting for something. Had he noticeably shuddered? No, he knew better than that. He never gave away his emotions.

Trina or Chloe must have asked a question. He felt some warmth at the jut of his cheekbones.

"Sorry," he said. His voice came out a little husky. Shutting down the dark images he'd just seen wasn't easy. "My mind was wandering."

"I asked if you'd like more chili." Trina nodded at his empty bowl.

"Oh, uh, thanks. I don't think so. It'll make a great lunch tomorrow."

She nodded and smiled at Chloe. "Ready for a bath?"

"Yes!" The little girl scrambled off her chair. When she hit the floor, her shoes flashed with neon pink lights. Gabe had bought them for her, thinking she'd like them. He'd seen her dance, staring entranced at her feet until she tripped over them and went down, giggling.

"Okay, just let me at least get started on cleaning up—"

"Nope." Gabe pushed back his chair. "You cooked, I clean."

"You'll put the chili away?"

He raised an eyebrow. "Don't trust me?"

A strange, almost frightened expression crossed Trina's face. But then she bit her lip, met his eyes and said, "Of course I do."

Disturbed, he watched as she hustled Chloe out of the kitchen. Exactly what kind of trust had they been talking about there?

TRINA DIDN'T KNOW what had gotten into her. This was ridiculous. She and Gabe had had great sex. Why not have more of it? She'd known from the beginning that she'd be risking heartbreak, but would another night, even another week's worth of nights, leave her more wounded than she'd already be?

Probably not. An involuntary sigh escaped her as she sank down on the edge of the tub and started the water running, then poured in the fragrant liquid that immediately frothed into giant, iridescent bubbles.

"Where's my mermaid?" Chloe stared in dismay at the array of toys in the basket beside the tub. Her worry ratcheted up. "I want my mermaid!"

For a man who'd never had kids or, from the sound of it, a little sister, Gabe had flawless taste in toys and clothes. Chloe loved everything he'd bought her. Trina might have suggested going for somewhat less girly, but then he'd brought the barnyard and alphabet puzzles. Before their ride this morning, he'd said in a low voice, "Do you think she'd like cowboy boots?"

Trina had rolled her eyes and said, "Is pink her favorite color?"

He'd laughed, the wonderful, deep rumble that had begun to sound less rusty than it had when they first came here.

Oh, heavens—were there such a thing as pink cowboy boots? Of course there were.

Trina delved in the basket, spotted a bit of yellow— why did mermaids never have plain brown hair?—and plucked out the rubber mermaid. "Voilà!"

Chloe seized her toy and stood obediently still while Trina peeled off her sweatshirt and pink overalls. Lifting them, Trina took a whiff. "Do I smell horse?"

The three-year-old giggled again. "I rode Mack today!"

"So you did. Hmm. Do you think I smell horsie?"

Chloe leaned toward her and sniffed ostentatiously. "Uh-huh."

"I bet Gabe does, too." Trina wondered if he'd shower before he went to bed, or wait until morning. She might discourage him. Horse was a nice addition to essence of man.

Chloe climbed into the tub and played contentedly while Trina watched her and tried to figure out what she could do or say to persuade her to talk about what she'd seen when her father was killed in front of her hideout.

What if, after all this, she said she'd seen a man, but she didn't know him? Maybe offered a vague description of brown hair that wasn't *almost* black like her daddy's, except, well, she couldn't really remember?

Except… Trina didn't believe that's what would happen.

Hearing a murmur of voices, Trina tensed, then realized Gabe must have turned on the TV. To watch the local news, undoubtedly. She made a habit of diverting Chloe so he could watch. The last thing they wanted was for her to see a recap of the awful crime that remained unsolved and had people in Sadler double-checking the locks on their doors.

Maybe Detective Risvold was right, and she should be pushing this child harder than she had been. Her instincts said no, but… Chloe had bounced back remarkably well, was exceptionally verbal for her age and seemed to have emerged from the shadow of fear.

Tomorrow, Trina decided. She'd come right out and ask. Did you see who hurt your daddy?

GABE FROWNED AT the television, entirely missing the byplay between the local news anchors. The pain that arced from one hip to the other told him he'd pushed too hard today in his workout. The last time he'd seen the physical therapist, the guy had lectured him.

"Some pain is productive, Gabe, but not all. You can do damage if you don't listen to what your body tells you."

He was damned if he'd listen. Because what his body was telling him was unacceptable. He'd worked through pain plenty of times before, and he would again this time.

A segment on the news caught his attention. A car had been turned into an accordion by a telephone pole. No way anybody in that vehicle had survived.

"Police don't yet know whether alcohol or drugs played a part in this tragedy," the reporter on scene told them earnestly. The flashing lights on police cars gave an eerie look to the backdrop. She gestured toward the torn hunk of metal that hardly resembled a car anymore. "It seems likely the driver far exceeded the speed limit, perhaps reaching eighty to a hundred miles an hour. As you can see—" the camera panned to the empty highway "—the road does curve here, which may explain why the driver lost control."

Gabe would have felt more pity if he hadn't thought how lucky it was that the dead man hadn't hit another car when he was flying down the highway. At least he hadn't killed anyone else.

Nothing else of interest came up. He paid attention to the weather report, but it held no surprises. He turned off the TV just as Trina hesitated at the foot of the stairs.

"Come and sit with me," he said.

She did, settling down on the sofa within the circle of his arm. Relieved, he bent his head to nibble on the rim of her ear. "Something's bothering you tonight."

"Oh… I guess I'm just frustrated." She told him what she'd been thinking, about pushing Chloe harder.

Gabe couldn't disagree, even as he felt reluctance he didn't understand. He wanted the two to be safe… but once an arrest was made, they wouldn't need to stay with him. His bodyguard stint would be done.

Or would it? Troubled, he thought about how ruthless drug trafficking organizations tended to be. Even if the killer was arrested, the trial wouldn't happen for months to years. What about the men who'd tried to shoot Gabe and his passengers out on the highway? He doubted the killer had been in that helicopter, either. Would those men ever be identified? There was some serious money behind this hunt for the little girl who could put away a man willing to murder to protect his illicit profits.

Assuming, he reminded himself, that the trafficking theory was accurate.

"What are you thinking?" Trina asked.

"If these are drug traffickers, I'm concerned that arresting the one man Chloe saw won't be enough."

He was sorry he'd said anything when he saw her face…and when his own thoughts took him to a logical conclusion.

He made sure he held Trina's gaze when he said,

"I take that back. If we're right that Pearson, Stearns or anyone else at Open Range is involved in transporting drugs, the traffickers will fold up their tent and find another way to move the drugs to markets. Right now they're trying to protect the guy who was useful because he'd developed a slick operation that may have been working for a long time. Who knows? Maybe even years. But reality is, once he goes down, the DEA will be all over O.R.E. The traffickers may already be trying to erase any footprint they've left there, just in case. If Chloe speaks out and can identify her father's killer, it's all over."

Trina's body jerked. "Maybe I should go wake her up and demand answers right this minute. Take her by surprise."

Gabe turned enough to wrap both arms around her. "You'd scare her. That wouldn't be a good start, and you know it."

She closed her eyes and let her head fall against his head. "I know. I keep thinking about this, though. If she'd seen a stranger, I'll bet Chloe would be able to tell us. She's talked about some really scary stuff."

"I think you're right," Gabe said. "On some level, she's torn. Whoever she saw, he's been around enough that she can't make herself believe—or accept—that he would hurt her daddy."

"Or she."

He inclined his head. "I may go back and talk to the neighbor who's attended parties at the Keifs' before. Who from O.R.E. was a regular at that house?"

He remembered the woman saying that Ron Pearson had been at one time—but not recently.

Trina stirred. "Given that Michael fired him, probably not Russell Stearns."

Gabe made an acknowledging noise in his throat, even as he wasn't thinking as sharply as he'd like. His hands had started roving, and he wanted to kiss her instead of continuing to talk. Would Trina be offended if he silenced her with his mouth?

With a small cry, she turned in his arms, pushed herself up so she was kneeling and pressed her mouth to his.

Urgency rose in him, hot and fast. He felt the sting of her teeth on his lip, and returned the favor. He gripped her butt and lifted her to straddle him. When she whimpered, he found her breast and kneaded. Damn, he was ready. It was like body-surfing a tsunami. Too powerful to be denied. Resenting any delay, he found himself struggling with the button and zipper on her chinos. He could free himself in seconds, but he had to get her out of her pants...

With a raw sound, Gabe ripped his mouth away from hers. "Chloe would see us if she came to the top of the stairs."

Those haunting eyes dazed, Trina blinked. Comprehension appeared slowly. "Oh, no."

"We have to make it upstairs."

She sat back on his thighs and traced the ridge under his zipper with one hand. "Think you can make it?"

When he snarled, she laughed.

"You'll pay for that," he muttered, rising with her clasped in his arms.

Her legs locked around his hips. "That sounds like fun."

He kissed her and, somehow, strode toward the stairs at the same time. If there was any buried pain left from his brutal workout, he didn't feel it.

EARLY THE NEXT AFTERNOON, Trina sat at the kitchen table rather than in the living room. She'd just put Chloe down for her nap and didn't want her voice drifting up the stairs to wake her.

Gabe had given her one of his burner phones, deciding it would be safe for her to make some calls with it, so long as she didn't contact the detectives. "Or," he'd added sternly, "anyone else who might possibly feel obligated to call them."

She knew he was restless. He wanted to be out there investigating in person, rather than from a distance. Prowling the trucking division of O.R.E., for example, or interviewing the woman who'd lunched with Russell Stearns. He had succeeded in identifying her from a photo on the company website. Julie Emmer, thirty-five, blonde and buxom, worked in accounting, a position that suggested the possibility she was using her creativity to disguise costs and income that the IRS, among others, might question. Trina had pointed out that Julie wasn't in a position to have masterminded illegal use of the trucks. If

Michael had suspected she was up to anything, why would he have hesitated to confront her, fire her—and call the cops?

Gabe hadn't disagreed. "When the feds step in, they're going to find a nest of vipers," he said. "No one man—or woman—is making this happen."

When he'd started pacing that morning, Trina suggested he borrow yet another vehicle and go do some detecting.

"We can't keep on this way, doing nothing but waiting," she'd exclaimed in frustration.

He'd scowled. "I don't see you leaning on Chloe yet."

"I just…had second thoughts." After last night's vehemence, she was embarrassed to have backpedaled today. "But when I see the right moment, I will."

"We've done more than wait," he argued. "I'd say we've made significant progress. Anyway, detectives spend most of their time on the phone and computer, not busting down doors or slamming suspects into walls."

Trina rolled her eyes. "At the very least, maybe you should talk to one of our favorite detectives again. You could tell him what you suspect. They might be willing to open up to you."

His scowl deepened. "I'm not leaving you alone."

Two hours later, he produced the phone. "Let me know the minute you're done. I'll destroy it."

She knew he'd talked to Boyd this morning, too. Boyd had been willing to be Gabe's legs on this, but they shared the concern that either could unintentionally lead the cops, if not the bad guys, right to the ranch.

Trina decided to call Vanessa again to ask about the helicopter. Gabe had determined online that the company did own two for the use of executives. He'd been unable to find a photo or description.

"The helicopters?" Vanessa sounded momentarily surprised. "Does this have anything to do about the one buzzing ranches?"

"I'm probably freaking about nothing, but when I saw the uproar on the morning news, I had to wonder if it could have anything to do with Chloe. You know why I'm worrying."

"I'll check with Bob and get back to you," the other woman said without questioning her further. "Oh, speaking of the news. Did you see anything about the guy who died when his car smashed into a telephone pole? He'd been a truck driver for O.R.E., and had quit his job that day. They're talking suicide."

"Really? There wasn't much of an update this morning."

"Online, there is. I saw his supervisor being interviewed by a reporter with News Channel 21," Vanessa informed her. "The supervisor tried to sound sorrowful, although I couldn't tell if it was genuine. He claimed Glenn Freeman had had an apparent breakdown, storming into the offices, talking wildly, threatening to kill himself and quitting. He acted like he was either drunk or stoned on something. The supervisor insisted he'd called Freeman's wife to express his concern. It was such a tragedy that the man took his own life before he could get help."

"Wow. I saw a mention of his death but not where he worked." Coincidence, anyone? "What did the wife have to say?"

"She was outraged. Glenn had been angry about something the previous evening, but he wasn't a heavy drinker and certainly didn't do drugs. She didn't believe for a minute that he'd have killed himself. Of course, spouses always do say that."

"True. It's interesting, though."

That was big enough news that Trina ventured out to find Gabe. Apparently, Boyd had produced the mysterious somebody who'd arrived this morning to replace the shattered window in Gabe's truck.

The two stood out by a white pickup talking. Boyd caught a glimpse of her coming out the back door and made a quick gesture. She retreated inside before the other man could see her.

She heard the sound of an engine, and Gabe followed her into the kitchen a minute later.

"Wasn't he supposed to see me?" she asked.

"I'm sure he's a good guy, but there's no point in taking chances."

Fine. "I just learned about something I thought you should know." She took a soda from the refrigerator and popped it open as she reminded him who Vanessa was, then asked if he'd read or seen anything about the high-speed car accident.

His attention sharpened. "I did last night, yeah."

"Well, Vanessa says he worked as a truck driver for O.R.E. The supervisor says he threw a scene when he quit, like he was drunk or on drugs. Now there's speculation that he drove himself into a telephone pole on his way home."

"That could be convenient for somebody."

"Apparently, the wife says he wasn't a heavy drinker, didn't use drugs and wasn't suicidal. She claimed he'd been upset or mad about something the evening before."

"Damn. I'd like to talk to her."

"Surely she'll tell the police if she knows anything. Plus, won't his car be examined to be sure it hadn't been tampered with?"

"It was destroyed. A mechanic might have trouble so much as finding a brake line."

"But why would he have been driving so fast?"

"I can think of a good reason," Gabe said softly.

Her breath caught. "Someone was in pursuit." She remembered the high speeds Gabe had reached, before he realized the enemy was in front of them as well as behind.

"Makes sense, doesn't it? Given whatever he likely spilled when he came in to quit, they couldn't afford to let him even make a phone call."

The poor man. Or maybe she should save her pity. It was possible he'd been knowingly transporting illegal drugs but made his employers mad by demanding more money, and even been foolish enough to try to blackmail a dangerous organization.

Her phone rang. Surprised, she saw that the caller was Vanessa. She mouthed the name to Gabe, who nodded.

"I made an excuse to call Bob," the other woman said, without preamble. "I mentioned what I saw about a helicopter flying low over local ranches and stampeding cattle, and he said the pilot must have been crazy to fly that low. I wondered where the helicopter could have come from, and he said, well, not from O.R.E. He's used company helicopters a couple of times to get to meetings in Portland. Theirs are white with the logo covering both sides."

Trina had seen the logo plenty of times. It had what looked like a Texas longhorn bursting through a circle. "Um…he didn't get curious about your interest?"

"No, he kind of volunteered the information. Besides the search and rescue and medic helicopters, the only other one he knew of belongs to the company that takes tourists sightseeing. You've seen it, haven't you?"

"I'd forgotten, but yes. It was painted bright orange, as I recall."

"Really garish," Vanessa agreed. "Listen, if there's anything else I can help with…"

They ended up leaving it at that. Once Gabe trashed this phone, Vanessa would have no way to reach her again. Of course, Trina hadn't told her that.

Setting the phone on the table, Trina said, "It has to be about O.R.E., doesn't it?"

"It's looking that way." His blue eyes never left her face. "You know what you have to do, Trina."

"Can we go see the foals first?" she begged. "Once she wakes up?"

He'd made excuses not to ride this morning. Out of Chloe's hearing, he said, "They're zeroing in on us. I'm reluctant to take you and Chloe out where you'd be exposed."

Now she thought, *Open range*. There was an irony.

After a moment he nodded. "I did offer. But… do you really expect her to be that traumatized by a few questions?"

"You saw her last time."

"I did, but she was downright perky by the time she'd had breakfast the next morning."

Trina slumped. "I'm a coward. I don't even know why! I work every day with kids and adults like her. I know we won't get anywhere until they tell me what's at the heart of their fear or depression. When they finally do, it's a cleansing hurt. It will be for Chloe, too. Even so—" She couldn't finish.

Gabe reached across the table to enclose her hand in his much larger one. "Sure you know why," he said, voice deep and comforting.

Her vision a little blurry, she tried to smile. "I love her."

"It makes all the difference."

A hard squeeze in her chest made her wonder. How did he know that, if he'd never let himself love anyone?

Was there any chance at all that *she'd* made a difference?

Chapter Twelve

Cross-legged on the sofa in the living room, Trina faced a child who sat with her head hanging. Chloe had been so joyful since seeing the dams and foals, helping hand out carrots and even touching the soft, inquisitive lips of a nearly snow-white foal. With just a few words, Trina had erased all that happiness. And yet how could she back off?

"Chloe, this is really important." For all that she was trying for her usual warmth and calm, urgency leaked through. "You saw somebody with your dad that morning, didn't you? The police don't know who hurt your mom and dad and brother."

Chloe sneaked a desperate peek at her before ducking her head again.

"We won't be able to go home until you tell me."

Right. Guilt would help.

Regretful, Trina cupped the little girl's chin, nudging it upward. "Honey?"

Suddenly, Chloe threw herself backward. "I don't

got a home!" she screamed, rolled off the couch and ran.

She wouldn't go outside by herself, would she? Adrenaline flooding her, Trina leaped up, too. Chloe had raced into the kitchen. The sound of a scraping at the back door electrified Trina. She came in sight just in time to see Gabe coming into the house, and scooping up Chloe, who'd aimed for the opening.

His alarmed gaze met Trina's. He didn't have to ask what had happened, because he knew what she intended when she led Chloe to the living room.

"Hey." He bounced her in his arms. "Hey. It's okay. It's okay."

Trina got a heart-stopping glimpse of Chloe's face, wet with tears…even as not a single sound escaped her lips.

Déjà vu.

GABE WOULD HAVE SWORN the kid had shrunk, and she'd already been tiny enough. She sat at the kitchen table only because Trina had plunked her down on her chair. She might as well have been a rag doll. She hadn't so much as glanced at the macaroni and cheese on the plate in front of her.

"Please, will you eat?" Trina begged. "It's your favorite food."

They all knew that. Earlier, she had promised to make Chloe's favorite dinner. She'd served peas tonight, too, another favorite.

And damn it, Gabe was hungry, and he liked macaroni and cheese, too, especially Trina's homemade version, but eating when Chloe looked so woeful didn't feel right. Trina hadn't taken more than a few bites, either.

Finally, she sighed. "If I dish up some ice cream, will you eat that?"

There wasn't a twitch to acknowledge her.

As protective as he felt for both of them, this was killing him. The little girl, shoved back into silence. The misery on Trina's face. She shouldn't have to shoulder responsibility for something they'd agreed needed to be done. Should he have joined her when she tried to get Chloe to open up? Maybe his presence would have reassured the scared child.

Or not.

He thought some nasty swear words. Now what? A bath? Would Chloe just sit in the water, instead of splashing happily the way she usually did? Would she sleep tonight, or huddle in darkness, feeling as if she were back in that cupboard waiting for her mommy to say it was okay to come out?

He cleared his throat. "Hey, munchkin. I need to give Mack some grain. Would you like to come out with me while Trina dishes up ice cream for all of us? Oats are Mack's idea of dessert, you know."

Chloe shook her head without looking at him.

Well, at least she was present. Gabe lifted a shoulder to say, *I tried.*

"You know what?" asked Trina, trying for false cheer. "I'm going to put your mac and cheese back, since you didn't touch it. There'll be plenty for us to have for lunch tomorrow."

"I wouldn't mind that ice cream," he said. "I bought chocolate mint, didn't I?"

Chloe pushed her lower lip out a fraction, just to be sure he didn't think he could soften her up. A hint of amusement lifted the weight in his chest by an ounce or two. He admired stubbornness.

Gabe rose to dish up the ice cream while Trina cleared the table, covered the casserole dish and put it in the fridge. When they passed each other, he kissed her on her cheek. "I predict a recovery by morning," he murmured.

Hope and doubt mixed on her face. "You think…?"

"She's going to be really hungry." He raised his voice. "Shall I dish some up for you, Chloe? Nope? Okay."

The kid held out and didn't watch the two adults eat their ice cream, but he had no doubt she was aware of every delicious, chilly bite going into their mouths. Once Trina held out a spoonful.

"Want a taste?"

Chloe crossed her arms and turned her face away.

Relief was beginning to loosen his unhappiness. He'd have called this a sulk, if Chloe's earlier panic and grief hadn't been obviously genuine. Nevertheless, he suspected that he and Trina were now being punished.

Sad to say, he thought ruefully, her attempt was working.

Twenty minutes later, Trina gave up and put on a

movie for Chloe, then came back to the kitchen. "I can't believe I blew it so badly!"

Gabe wrapped her in a comforting embrace and kept his voice low. "You keep saying that, but I don't know why. Maybe she's not ready to talk. That doesn't make asking questions wrong."

"It's the way I did it. I let my frustration get to me. I know better. I do."

Feeling a smile growing on his face, Gabe said, "Hadn't occurred to me before, but I think I used the same technique Chloe did to get rid of those damn therapists at the hospital that kept trying to make me open up about my feelings."

Trina pushed back from him. "You became catatonic?"

"No, I got sullen."

"Did it work?"

"Absolutely." Somewhere, he found a grin, even though the subject had been a sore one and this day had sucked. "I wasn't real enthusiastic about you, you know, once Joseph told me what you did for a living."

"I did notice," she said tartly.

"Although—" his smile faded and he found himself looking into her eyes "—somehow you've gotten a lot further than any of them did."

"Really?" It was a whisper.

"Really." He cleared his throat for the second time this evening, and for the same reason. Emotions trying to choke him. What was he going to do about her?

"I might have wanted to get into your head," she

said, still so quietly he barely heard her, "but I've never tried to offer therapy."

"Do you think I need it?"

She frowned but shook her head. "No. And certainly never from me."

It felt like a promise. An important one. Gabe thought about saying something but finally settled for a nod. Trina gave him a shaky smile and retreated.

"I hate to say this, but I think I should stay with her tonight. I don't like the idea of her being alone."

He didn't want to be alone, either, but he was a lot less fragile than Chloe, so he nodded.

When Trina took Chloe upstairs for her bath a few minutes later, he didn't follow, even though he wanted to. He liked listening to Chloe playing in the tub, Trina teasing her. More often than he'd want Trina to know, he stood in the hall and listened to her read picture books and fairy tales aloud, taking on the voices of characters. He'd have liked to see the expressions on her face, too. If he'd gone in to join them, would she have felt too silly to squeak and rumble and whisper?

Tonight, it felt damn lonely down here.

USUALLY, CHLOE WAS a snuggler. Even sound asleep, she made her way across the bed when Trina got into it. Maybe she was only drawn to warmth, Trina didn't know.

Tonight, Chloe had curled up on her side facing the window. When Trina gently rubbed her back beneath the covers, she'd subtly arched away, reminding Trina of how a cat shrank from a touch.

"I'm sorry," Trina whispered. "I know I got really pushy today. I wish I could see what you saw, and never have to ask you." She waited, hoping Chloe would do or say something, but the small lump didn't move. "While you're falling asleep," she murmured, "think about the horses. Wasn't that foal beautiful? You heard Gabe say he'll end up dappled and gray the way his mommy is, but that's beautiful, too. I think the foal was curious, because you were small like him."

Closing her eyes but knowing sleep would be slow coming, Trina saw Gabe's face instead of horses. And his big, graceful body. She was almost painfully conscious of him whenever he was near. She'd thought actually having sex would vent some of the tension, but it hadn't.

Twice in her life—leaving out early teenage crushes—she'd thought she was in love, but those feelings hadn't been anything like this deep longing, physical and emotional. She knew she was probably deluding herself to think he felt something similar, that he might be questioning the certainties about his future that he'd thought rock solid.

Her mood bleak, she wondered if she might be sorry if she got what she was wishing for. If they were serious about each other, what would she do? Move to the army base where he was stationed, try to find work and then wave a falsely cheerful goodbye every time he shipped out? Wait for weeks and months and even a year at a time for him to come back to her, haunted the entire while by fear that he'd be injured again—or come back in a box to be buried? Even if she loved him, was that a life she could endure?

He'd said himself that he wouldn't be an active-duty Ranger for that much longer. But what did that mean? Two more years? Five? Ten?

Yet if she loved him, how could she not accept him for what he was, be waiting when he came home?

And, of course, all this agonizing was absurd when she didn't have the slightest idea how he felt about her, or whether any new emotions had the slightest impact on his determination to rejoin his unit. Trina didn't even know why he loved being a Ranger so much. Was it the sense of mission? The danger, the exhilaration of cheating death? The tightness with his teammates? Would he ever talk to her about it?

Sleep sneaked up on her. She roused when Gabe came up to bed, listened to every small sound from his bedroom, even toyed with the idea of slipping out of bed and going to him. But her eyelids were so heavy, and tonight she didn't want Chloe to wake and find herself alone.

She must have slept like a log, because her next conscious awareness was of morning light seeping around the edges of the blinds. And of the bony knees pressing against her stomach, and the warm little girl who'd wormed her way beneath Trina's arm.

Trina's lips curved as she stayed absolutely still.

Yesterday had been a setback, that's all. Everyone made mistakes; everyone got scared sometimes. She remembered Gabe predicting a recovery by morning. Oh, she hoped he was right!

Finally, her bladder drove her to get up. Inevitably, Chloe woke up, too, blinking sleepily at her.

Trina swooped down to kiss her cheek, said, "Good morning, sunshine!" and dashed across the hall to the bathroom. On the way back, she glanced at Gabe's door, ajar, but couldn't tell if he was still in bed or long since up.

Returning to the bedroom, she found Chloe sitting on the side of the bed, clutching her plush unicorn. Still cheerfully, she said, "I'll bet you're hungry, aren't you?" Her own stomach was growling. "Let me get dressed, and let's go make breakfast. How about oatmeal? That'd fill us up."

Predictably, Chloe wrinkled her nose. "Can we have waffles?"

Trina's heart felt as if it was swelling to fill her rib cage. "Yep. If you want to help, you need to get dressed, too."

Chloe scampered to the bathroom first. On her return, she picked out red corduroy overalls and a pink shirt, a combination that made Trina wince, but what the heck? "Can we ride *today*?" she asked, while sitting on the floor putting on socks.

Trina looked for Chloe's shoes. "I don't know. I think Gabe is nervous because of that helicopter coming overhead. Since we're hiding here, he wants to make sure nobody sees us."

A sock halfway on, Chloe went still. Yesterday, Gabe hadn't been honest with Chloe about why they couldn't go, but creative excuses would collapse eventually. Right now she and Trina were pretty much cabin-bound, and Chloe already knew why, more or less.

The little girl looked up. "Why can't *this* be home?" she asked, voice small and plaintive. "Can't we stay here? With Gabe?"

Oh, God. Trina wanted that so fiercely the pain held her silent for a moment. Finally, she swallowed, crouched beside Chloe, and kissed her on the forehead. "I like it here, too. But...your grandma might want you to live with her. Remember?"

"I don't wanna go live with her!" Chloe wrapped her arms around Trina's calf and held on tight. "I want you to be my mommy!"

I want to be your mommy, too. But she couldn't say that, because it might not be possible. Probably wouldn't be. Chloe *had* relatives.

Had it been another, terrible mistake, letting herself love this child, when she knew she wouldn't be able to keep her?

Maybe. But it wasn't one she'd take back if she could. No, she thought, on a wave of peace salted with pain, loving Gabe wasn't something she'd take back, either.

Struggling to calm herself, she said, "You know

I love you, sweetie. Right now we're sort of…waiting to see what will happen. I can't make you promises, except that, if you go live with your grandma or your aunt and uncle, I'll come see you as often as I can. Okay?"

Chloe's face crumpled, but she nodded.

"Waffles," Trina declared, spotting the missing shoes tucked just beneath the bed.

As GABE AND MACK loped toward Boyd's house, he was stuck on thinking about what Trina had told him. Chloe's extreme reaction had happened not because she was afraid to talk about the bad man, but because she didn't want to go "home."

"That was a stupid thing for me to say, anyway." Trina was way too quick to berate herself for anything she viewed as a screwup. "Even *I* don't have a home. Chloe knows that. Hers is just a nightmare. She must have been thinking she was safe here, but that once we leave, she'll have to go live in a strange house with a relative she doesn't know that well."

It bugged Gabe to know that might well be true. How could Trina combat it if family wanted to take her in? His heart had done some strange acrobatics when he heard that Chloe wanted them to stay here, with *him*. So far, he was mostly ignoring the small voice in the back of his head that said, *They could if you retire.*

If he surrendered to a damn injury, was what he meant. The idea was unthinkable to a man who'd made himself without a lot of encouragement or support from anyone else. He didn't *quit*.

Except...hell. He really didn't like imagining the day Trina thanked him and he had to hug her and Chloe goodbye because they were going on with their lives.

Alone under an overcast sky, he said a word he had had to swallow a few times recently because he didn't want a three-year-old kid to hear it...and because he was old-fashioned enough not to like using it around a woman, either.

When he reached the bustling heart of the ranch, he rode Mack into a barn, dismounted and tied him there, in the relatively cool, dim aisle lined by stalls. He had to stop and talk to a man holding a horse out front while a farrier bent over working on a front hoof. Then he walked toward the house, where Boyd expected him.

"You made it," his partner said, letting him in.

"You thought I'd get lost?"

"Hey, you never know. Haven't seen much of you around here."

"You know why," he said, too sharply, when he knew Boyd was only kidding. Man, this never-ending tension was getting to him, in large part because he wanted to take action. He wanted to find the bastard who was behind all this crap, not wait to *be* found. And yeah, he didn't like that Boyd had been able to go out and do things he couldn't, even though this was another kind of teamwork.

He accepted an offer of iced tea, and the two men

sat in the enormous living room. Gabe felt uncomfortable in such a large space. He'd be curious to see whether Trina preferred this showplace of a log home.

Boyd said abruptly, "The Keifs' neighbor didn't recognize Julie Emmer." She was the accountant Gabe had seen having lunch with Russell Stearns. "I showed her the photo on my phone, and she kept shaking her head. This Julie hadn't been to any of the same parties she had."

He nodded.

"I may have left Mrs. Freeman thinking I was a reporter. When I said I had questions about her husband and his death, she let me in without asking for ID."

Not smart, but not uncommon, either. The woman's life had just been smashed.

"She insisted Glenn hadn't told her what was worrying him about his work, but something was. She said it had started two or three days before he died. He'd had a short run—Seattle—and came home really upset. She thought something might have happened on the road, but he said not. He told her he couldn't keep working for O.R.E., that he was sorry because they might have to move and the kids would hate getting pulled from school."

Gabe winced. The television reporter had described him as "a married father of two children," but he hadn't really thought of the poor kids. "What about her interviews with the cops? Did they sound aboveboard?"

"I'm going to say no." Boyd's expression was grim.

"She said the detective asked only whether Glenn had been drinking too much, whether he'd sought counseling. Could he have had a car accident he hadn't told her about, maybe a string of tickets? That might have made him fear he'd be fired. Did he sometimes speed?"

"In other words, this detective steered away from anything that might point to a problem at O.R.E."

"You got it. In fairness, the company is the biggest employer in the county, by a long shot. I'm going to guess local government in general tiptoes around O.R.E. issues."

Gabe grunted. That was, of course, an explanation for some of Risvold's problems investigating the Keifs' murders.

"When I raised the subject of drugs," Boyd continued, "she flipped out. What was I talking about? And then she got mad and said Glenn wouldn't have been involved with anything so vile." He grimaced. "She showed me the door."

"Damn. If only he'd told her what he'd discovered."

"That would be nice," Boyd countered, "except that if there'd been any hint he had in her first response to the news about her husband, I doubt she'd have lived long."

"No, you're right." Gabe stretched out his legs and gazed broodingly at his booted feet. "Her obvious shock and ignorance saved her."

Boyd stayed silent, a frown pulling at his eyebrows. After a while, he said, "So, what's next?"

"Hell if I know." Gabe told him about Trina's attempt to put some pressure on Chloe, and how it had backfired.

Sounding tentative, unusual for him, Boyd began, "If you three just stay hunkered down..."

Gabe swore and surged to his feet. Glaring down at his friend, he said, "Until Chloe's ready to start kindergarten? I think Trina's partners might have kicked her out of the practice by then, don't you? And what happens after my physical?"

He made a rough sound and shoved his fingers through hair that was way past regulation length, bracing himself to be called out on the dramatics.

All Boyd said was, "You still working out?"

His glare probably intensified. "Of course I am!"

"And?"

"And what?" Gabe snarled, but he knew. Would he pass the physical? He hated feeling conflicted about the possible outcome. Damn, did he *want* to fail, because of these inconvenient feelings for a woman?

His buddy smiled faintly. "Okay."

"I've got to get back. I don't like leaving them." He'd just felt a tug, as if he were attached with a tether.

"I understand." Without further comment, Boyd walked him out.

Gabe mounted, trotted Mack out of the barn and kicked him almost immediately into a gallop.

TRINA TOOK THE containers holding the peas nobody had eaten last night and the mac and cheese, too, from the refrigerator. This was one meal that couldn't be easier. Of course, she shouldn't get ahead of herself, assuming Gabe would rush home. He and Boyd might have a lot to talk about—

A neigh from outside drew her to the window, where she could see the paddock, where the gelding she'd been riding called eagerly over the fence. Yes! Coming into sight, Mack answered, and Gabe leaned forward to slap him on the neck.

She went into the living room, unnerved when she didn't immediately see Chloe. She rushed to the downstairs bathroom, calling, "Chloe?"

The bathroom was empty. Trina spun to go for the stairs but spotted Chloe crawling out from behind a hefty leather easy chair.

"It scared me when I didn't see you. Were you hiding?"

"Kinda." Her eyes were red, her hair stringy and falling out of the ponytail.

Trina sank down on the chair and held out her hand. "Will you come and cuddle with me?" To heck with lunch.

The little girl sniffed, nodded and, with a little help, scrambled up onto Trina's lap. Trina tucked her in close and resolved not to ask any more questions. The comfort of an embrace was enough.

Chloe mumbled something Trina didn't hear. She

bent her head closer, even as she half listened for the back door to open.

"I sawed Uncle Ronald."

It took a few seconds for the words to sink in. Chloe had sawed—seen—a man she called "uncle." Ronald.

"'Cept, *he* wouldn't hurt Daddy!" she exclaimed passionately. "He leaned over so I sawed him. He musta been going to help Daddy get up, only…only he didn't."

"Oh, honey."

Chloe sounded younger, as if she'd regressed in the past few minutes to a time when her language was less well developed. The tear-wet, freckled face peered up at Trina in bewilderment.

"I *almost* went out, but then I 'membered Mommy saying to wait, no matter what, so I didn't."

Trina sent a prayer of thanks winging upward. She wished Chloe's mother could know that she had saved her. Maybe…maybe she did.

"I'm so glad," she whispered. "So glad."

Chloe muffled a sob against her.

The creak of a floorboard brought Trina's head up fast. Gabe stood in the opening from the kitchen, his expression arrested. Swallowing the agony and the hope, she nodded.

Chapter Thirteen

"Call me paranoid," Gabe growled, "but I don't trust Risvold in particular. He may have innocent reasons for his behavior and his excuse for an investigation, but I can't forget that he or his department had a leak." Remembering the burns on Trina's back spiked his temper. That fire had come damn close to claiming two victims, ensuring that the Keif murders were never solved.

Despite all Gabe had seen and done, he had to shake his head over this guy. Ronald Pearson had to be unbelievably cold-blooded and ruthless. The same could be said about the terrorists Gabe hunted, but they at least committed atrocities out of idealism, however mistaken, not greed.

"You're right," Trina said in response to his reminder. "But...a detective? I did some research online, and he's been with the Sadler Police Department for twelve years."

"Detective for six of those. I know. And he might have been accepting kickbacks for those same twelve years," Gabe pointed out. "Longevity and integrity aren't synonymous."

She made a face. "What are you going to tell them, then?"

Gabe rolled his shoulders to release some tension. "To start with, I'll call Deperro, not Risvold. I won't accuse his partner of anything, but I'll express our concern about the past leak that was damn near fatal for you and Chloe." Concern being such a pallid word for what he really felt.

Trina shivered. "Yes, it was."

"I'll set up a meeting for them to ask Chloe their questions." They both knew the cops couldn't make an arrest based on the word of an anonymous caller. Not Trina's word, either. No, they'd insist on interviewing the three-year-old witness.

Sounding uneasy, Trina said, "You mean, take her to town?"

"Not a chance." He made his voice solid granite. "They could grab her and we couldn't stop them. I'm thinking at Boyd's place. We can make sure there are too many witnesses for them to be able to get away with anything."

Her fingers bit into her palms. "Does that mean we can stay here, then? Until it's all over? I mean, they wouldn't know the cabin is here, or your name…"

"I'm on the deed and there's a permit on file for the cabin," he said, almost gently. "And don't forget the flyover. It wouldn't take a genius to realize that, if we know Boyd, this or one of the other ranch houses is a good possibility for the hideout."

Her anxiety wasn't as well hidden as she probably thought it was, but she only nodded. "Then we'll have to figure out something else."

Moving fast, he shoved back his chair and rounded the table. Gripping her upper arms, he tugged her to his feet. "I won't abandon you."

She blinked a couple of times in quick succession, nodded and softened, letting herself lean against him. He wanted to share his strength with her but knew that wasn't why she needed him. This was a gutsy woman. Despite the intense compassion that allowed her to reach terrified children, she'd do whatever she had to.

She straightened and stepped back, even managing a smile of sorts. "Thank you. I...had faith that you wouldn't. So, are you going to Bend again?"

He'd rather still be holding her but respected her decision to stand on her own two feet. "Yeah, I think so. If they've ever traced one of my calls, with luck they'll think we're in that area."

"Okay. I'd tell you to get groceries, too, but we don't need anything."

"Good. I don't want to be away that long." He smiled crookedly. "Although I do appreciate my home-cooked meals."

She chuckled. "Are you running out of phones yet?"

"Nope, I pick one up every time I go in the right

kind of store. Better not to be remembered as the guy who purchased ten phones. Speaking of, I'm going to leave one with you, in case of an emergency. I'll enter my number, Boyd's and Leon Cabrera's. One or both of them may be closer than I am."

Whether he liked it or not, the possibility was real that bad stuff could go down at any time.

"You'd better get going," she suggested.

"Yeah." After entering the numbers, Gabe handed a phone to her. Then he kissed her, quick and hard, and went out the door. He heard her lock it behind him before he strode to the outbuilding where he garaged his truck.

Having decided not to take the time to switch out vehicles, Gabe spent the drive second-guessing himself. Would a recording of Chloe's testimony be sufficient? That's all a jury would see, anyway. No one would put a preschooler on the stand. Or was there a safer place for a meet, one that wouldn't give away their location?

But he shook his head at that. It wouldn't surprise him if the cops already knew where they were. To give them a strong suspicion, all they'd have had to do was succeed in tracing one of those assorted license plates to a guy now working at the ranch.

He really did believe that the rats would desert the sinking ship the minute cuffs closed around Ronald Pearson's wrists. He and Trina would need to stay on guard for a while, sure, but—

A Deschutes County Sheriff's Department car

passed him going the other direction, a sight that snapped him back to the awareness of his surroundings. He knew better than to brood at the wrong time and place.

Ten minutes later, he parked, facing out, in the Home Depot lot.

His call was put through to the detective, who answered brusquely. "Deperro."

"Detective, this is Dr. Marr's friend."

"Damn it, what's with the secrecy?"

"You know as well as I do," he snapped. "You have a leak. If you know how word got out about Chloe starting to talk and where she was living, you should have told Dr. Marr or me. As it is, I don't figure I can talk to either of you without assuming what I say may be passed on."

"That's insulting."

Gabe's radar hummed. Deperro should have spoken sharply; *sounded* insulted. Instead, he'd said what he ought to, but without conviction.

"I have news," Gabe said abruptly. "Chloe told Trina and me who she saw that morning. It was the partner, Ronald Pearson." He heard only silence. Stunned? "'Uncle Ronald' is what she called him. He bent over her father's body, so she got a good look at his face. She thought he was going to help her daddy get up, but he didn't."

"Damn," Deperro muttered.

Gabe could think of stronger words. "If you're doing your job, by now you know the likelihood that drug traffickers are using O.R.E.'s fleet of trucks to transport their products to market. Chances are that Michael Keif found out somehow, and they had a confrontation."

"Risvold doesn't believe in the drug angle, but I was heading that direction."

"Good to know. Okay. I'm assuming you need to talk to Chloe yourself before you can make an arrest."

"Yeah." The detective's voice sounded hoarse. "We do. Man. I've never arrested anyone based on the word of a kid that age."

"Now that you know, you'll find plenty of other evidence. I hope you have the DEA ready to close in on Open Range the second you've arrested the bastard."

Possibly irritated, the guy only said, "Will you bring the girl here? The sooner, the better. What time?"

"Not there. I need better security than you can give us." He mentioned the local rancher he knew, who had agreed to allow them to meet at his house. "We can do this afternoon. We'll need an hour or two to get there, be prepared."

They agreed on four o'clock. Gabe glanced at the dashboard clock. Yeah, that gave them plenty of time. He named Boyd and the ranch, then ended the call.

Once again, he dumped the phone on his way out of the parking lot, this time in a small, wrinkled bag left from an order of burgers and fries. Then he steered a route to the highway.

TRINA DID A lot of pacing even as she listened for any sound from Chloe upstairs. She felt again as if her skin had shrunk, only worse.

It wasn't as if there was any reason to think they were in danger, unless... Was he right, that the detectives might have figured out how to find them? If so, they'd displayed more patience than she would have anticipated. Their initial impatience had been understandable. How frustrating would it be to have a single witness and she was not only mute but couldn't communicate by writing, either? Had they actually come to grasp how traumatized Chloe was? Remembering her last conversation from Risvold, she made a face.

Not feeling any calmer, Trina went from window to window, stealing looks out. The only movement was in back, where the horses wandered from the paddock into the shade of an overhang where Gabe kept a manger and a tub of water. Finally, surrendering to this edgy feeling, she opened the gun safe. She could just leave it standing open... No, she couldn't. What if she didn't see Chloe come downstairs? Okay, then, she'd take out the black rifle Gabe had let her handle as well as the smallest handgun, and set them up high on the bookshelves, where she could snatch them quickly at need. She knew he'd checked, and rechecked, to be sure they were loaded and ready if she needed them.

She felt a little better once she had the guns out and had closed the safe again securely. Then she went back to her route, window to window, and to clock-watching.

Gabe would have made his call and started back. More than that—he'd surely be home in fifteen to twenty minutes, if he hadn't been held up. Say, he'd had to wait to reach the detective.

Ten minutes later, the sound of an engine came to her. Trina almost slumped in relief, but she went to the front window and opened a slit in the blinds to see out. Dust rose on the cutoff to Gabe's cabin. The vehicle was big and black...but something didn't look quite right. Wary, she waited.

It was an SUV that pulled up in front, one with the kind of antennas that police cars had. And a row of lights inside, at the top of the windshield. A man got out.

Detective Risvold. She could make out his face clearly, see the badge on his belt and the holstered gun at his hip. Why would he have just showed up here like this?

Apprehensive, Trina took out the phone, went to Gabe's number, then changed her mind. Boyd was closer. Her thumb hovered over the screen.

"Ms. Marr!" Risvold called. At least he had the sense to wait by his SUV. "I know you're in there. I'm here to talk to the girl."

He couldn't know anything of the kind, not for sure.

Ignore him? Crack the door and tell him he had to wait?

Call Boyd. But for a second, she hesitated. Had she heard something upstairs? *Don't let Chloe come down, not now.*

"Damn it, Miss... *Dr.* Marr." He leaned on the "doctor." Sneering? Or pacifying her? "I'm short on patience. There's a killer walking free. I can't do anything about that until I hear what the kid has to say."

All true.

Ring. Ring. Ring. Finally, "Chaney here."

"It's Trina," she whispered, then realized there wasn't any reason not to speak in a normal voice. "Detective Risvold is standing out front demanding I let him in to interview Chloe."

"What?" Boyd said. "How the hell did he find you? Never mind. Damn, I'm on horseback, probably ten minutes from home, longer to get to you. Where's Gabe?"

"He drove to Bend to call. He told you what Chloe said?"

"Yeah. Shit. Don't let the guy in. I'll call Leon. He may be nearer to you."

"Okay. Thank you. Gabe should be back anytime."

"Good. You armed?"

"Yes, but... I can't shoot a police officer!"

"You can if he takes out a window or tries to break in," he said grimly. "Go for a warning shot. That ought to have him retreating out of range."

Her smile wobbled. "Okay. Thanks, Boyd." She sidled over to the bookcase and grabbed the rifle. She was more comfortable with it. Then she scrolled to Gabe's number, just as more dust rose outside as another vehicle approached fast. Was he back...?

No, this was a dark gray sedan with, she saw as it got closer, the same kind of antenna.

She pushed Send.

GABE'S HANDS CLENCHED in frustration on the steering wheel as he sat in his truck in the scant shade of a lodgepole pine. After leaving Highway 97, he'd driven only a few miles on the secondary road before spotting a police car parked on a dirt pulloff ahead. Probably there to catch a few speeders, but he couldn't risk sailing by. It was unlikely the deputy would notice the distinctive dents made by bullets, but a BOLO with the description of Gabe's truck or the license plate might conceivably have gone out. Gabe had been lucky enough to see a dirt lane turning off to the left half a mile before he reached the cop, and he'd taken it.

A dusty plume rose behind the truck. He'd driven only until he passed out of sight over a rise before he braked and maneuvered until he was facing back the way he'd come. Then he drove slowly until he could see the damn cop.

Waiting, he felt his gut seething. He kept glancing at his phone. He could call Trina, but all he'd do was scare her.

On the highway, a pickup pulling a stock trailer

passed. Not a likely speeder. The police car stayed where it was.

His phone rang. He looked down at the strange number and knew. Trina.

IT WAS DETECTIVE DEPERRO who got out of the second car, Trina saw in surprise. Why wouldn't they have come together?

Advancing on his partner, Deperro didn't even glance at the house. He looked mad, she realized. Wanting to hear what they were saying, she grabbed the rifle and unlocked and cracked open the front door.

"…shouldn't have come." That was Risvold.

"We have a meeting set up. You know that. This—" the other detective's sweeping gesture including the cabin, the SUV and Risvold himself "—doesn't look good."

Risvold was sweating profusely. Half-turned as he was to face his partner, she thought he said, "I tried to keep you out of this."

Her uneasiness crystalized and she fumbled with the safety, then raised the barrel of the rifle, but too late. Risvold pulled his gun and shot Detective Deperro in the chest. Shock on his face, Deperro staggered back, fell.

Furious but also feeling weirdly calm, Trina sighted and shot out the window of the SUV. "Drop the gun!" she yelled.

Risvold wheeled toward her and fired. The *crack*

and *thud* when the bullet plowed into the heavy wooden door seemed simultaneous.

She fired back, probably a little wildly. The bullet skimmed the side of the SUV. Risvold swore viciously and leaped behind it.

She suddenly realized she couldn't see Deperro. Which meant he wasn't dead. He must have crawled, because he sure hadn't jumped to his feet; she'd have seen that. Maybe he and Risvold were *both* taking refuge behind the rear of the SUV, which wouldn't be good.

Gabe, please hurry. Boyd, where are you? But she knew, in some part of her mind, that hardly any time had actually passed.

"Trina?" A scared voice came from behind her.

Oh, God, of course the gunshots had awakened Chloe.

"Honey, I need you to—" No, no, she couldn't tell her to hide, to not come out until Trina or Gabe told her so. Once in a lifetime was enough. Except—Trina desperately wanted her to *have* a life. "Get down behind the couch," she said. "A man is shooting at the house, and I don't want him to hit you by accident."

The second she saw the little girl duck behind that hefty leather sofa, Trina turned back to peer through the crack again. Risvold...no sight of him. But Detective Deperro had somehow gotten up. Emerging from the other side of the SUV, he bent over and ran toward the far corner of the cabin.

Another shot rang out. He hit the ground, rolled

and grabbed his thigh. Trina fired again, this time aiming through the nonexistent windshield and out a side window, she hoped very close to where Risvold must be crouched. Right above his head would be good.

She heard swearing and fired again. Deperro staggered to his feet and kept going.

She had to ignore the whimper from behind the couch.

I'll run out of bullets, she realized, not quite as calmly. Gabe had said the Savage Model 110 had a four-cartridge box. Five shots, with one already loaded. She counted. How many times had she already fired? Three? No, four. One more. Then she'd have to go for the handgun.

A pounding at the back door had her lurching around. *Oh.* It had to be Boyd or Leon. She hesitated only an instant, made sure Risvold was still out of sight, closed and locked the door.

Ignoring the whimper from behind the sofa, she ran.

GABE DROVE LIKE a madman.

The sheriff's department car had suddenly pulled out onto the highway and accelerated. The rack of lights came on, red, white, blue, rotating. Boyd had said he'd call 911. Gabe hoped this deputy was on his way to the ranch.

But damn it, he turned off on a lonely crossroad and raced up over a rise.

From that moment on, Gabe floored it. He didn't slow down even when he groped for his ringing phone.

"Leon's out in hell-and-beyond to rescue a steer tangled in barbed wire," Boyd reported tensely. "I'm on my way, but close to ten minutes out. I'm hearing shots."

Gabe breathed a word that might have been a profanity or a prayer. Or both. "I might beat you there," he said. "I'll pass the cutoff, and approach from behind the cabin."

"Don't shoot me." Boyd was gone.

If that was meant to be funny, it missed its mark. The urgency driving Gabe left no room for humor.

THE KITCHEN DOOR had a glass inset. Rifle raised in firing position, Trina peered around the corner from the living room.

It was Detective Deperro looking to one side, then turning suddenly, as if he'd heard her, to stare right at her.

He raised a fist and mimicked knocking, even as he darted another look toward the far corner of the cabin.

Queasy, Trina couldn't help wondering if the fight out front had been a setup, designed to make her trust one of the two partners and let him in. What if that first bullet had been, she didn't know, a blank? But the second one...no, she'd seen blood blossom on Deperro's leg.

Wait. He must be wearing a bulletproof vest.

That's why the shot had knocked him down but not injured him significantly.

Make a decision.

It wasn't any kind of decision, she realized almost immediately. He could use the butt of his gun to knock out the glass so he could let himself in. In fact, he could have done that already, instead of waiting politely despite the stress and pain he must be feeling. Her only other option was to shoot him. Of course she couldn't do that.

A thought floated absurdly through her head. Gabe hadn't built his cabin to withstand a siege. She'd bet he was going to be sorry.

She rushed forward and unlocked the door, throwing it open.

Deperro flung himself in, and she saw that the leg of his cargo pants was soaked with blood.

"Oh, no. Did it hit an artery? You should lie down and elevate your leg." She sounded, and felt, hysterical.

His dark eyes met hers. "No, I wouldn't have made it this far if the artery was spurting. It hurts like a mother—" He censored himself. "But I'll live. Listen, we don't have time for this."

"No." Trina sprinted for the living room. Seeing Chloe huddled in a small ball, she stopped. "Sweetie, please go upstairs to the bedroom."

Except for the shivers, Chloe didn't move, didn't respond. Didn't even lift her head. Trina wanted to go to her but couldn't.

She hated that the closed blinds didn't let her see out front at all. After grabbing the handgun, she leaned the rifle against the wall beside the door.

A dragging footstep behind her was followed by the detective saying softly, "Well, hello, little one." Then, obviously speaking to Trina, "Where's the guy who's been calling me?"

"On his way. Here any minute." She had to believe that. She pressed her back to the door. "What happened?"

"Damn. You got some towels or something else I can use?"

"There's a bathroom under the staircase."

She watched him go, then undid the dead bolt, gripped the Colt and cracked the door, ready to shoot. Nothing happened. She peered out. No movement. But Risvold could be on the porch already. Without sticking her head out, she wouldn't see him if he was off five feet to one side or another. Holding her breath, she listened. The silence was absolute.

"I'm making a mess," Deperro said. "I'm sorry."

She checked over her shoulder. He'd ripped a towel lengthwise and somehow tied half of it around his thigh, the other half folded to provide a pad.

Her laugh broke. "That's the least of our problems."

"Yeah, it is." He was staring at the thin band of sunlight. "I've been wondering about Risvold, but... damn, I still can't believe he's crooked. I told him what your friend said, that we were meeting at four, and a couple of minutes later he made an excuse and sidled out. I followed him."

"But…what can he do by himself?"

Those eyes were now black, the set of his mouth grim. "I don't think he'll be by himself for long."

Suddenly light-headed, she wheeled to peer through the crack again, and saw a cloud of dust out on the road.

GABE'S TRUCK ROCKETED down the dirt road. He'd lowered the windows but didn't hear any shots. What if he was too late? What if he found Trina and Chloe— No, damn it! He wouldn't even think that.

He passed the cutoff to his cabin, drove another two or three hundred yards, then steered off the road, bumping over rough ground. He parked, leaped out and ran. He wasn't halfway to the cabin when he saw a cloud of dirt rising where his had just settled. Reinforcements? Bad enough that Trina was already having to face down two armed, experienced cops.

Unless she was dead, taken out by one of those shots.

He willed the fear away. With luck, Boyd had beaten him here.

He broke from the trees behind the paddock and barn. An engine—no, more than that, at least two— announced the approach of more vehicles. Mack and the gelding were snorting, moving restlessly but sticking close to the barn. Smart. Stepping lightly, Gabe eased around the corner to where he could see the back of the cabin. Nothing there. The door was still closed, the window intact.

A voice behind him said softly, "Yo, it's me."

He spun in a shooting position, his brain catching up in time to keep his finger from tightening on the trigger. Sweat darkened Boyd's hair and his T-shirt, creating a sheen on his face. He carried a handgun that he must have had with him in case of trouble.

"Has she called again?" Boyd asked.

"Not a word." Gabe pulled his keys from his pocket. "Ready?"

They didn't run, just moved as quietly as a pair of ghosts, sweeping the surroundings with their guns as they went. At the back door, Boyd covered him while Gabe unlocked it. They stepped inside. He immediately heard a man's voice. Son of a bitch.

He didn't even look at Boyd, just walked toward the living room without making a sound.

First, he saw Chloe, squeezed to try to make herself invisible. He evaluated her with lightning speed. Her whole body trembled. She didn't even look up. Scared out of her skull, but alive. Then he saw the man's back. Hair as dark as Leon's, but this guy was a lot bigger. He clearly hadn't heard the man approaching behind him.

Gabe measured the distance.

Chapter Fourteen

"It's an SUV." Trina spoke tensely. "Another one's coming behind it."

"Crap," Deperro muttered. "Why don't you let me take the front, you get where you can see the back door?"

"Don't shoot," a dark, deep voice said.

Trina spun and saw that Deperro had done the same. "It's Gabe!" she cried, having to stiffen her knees to keep from crumpling to the floor in relief.

His eyes met hers fleetingly, the expression so raw her heart skipped a beat. The next second, her personal warrior stared hard at the detective. "What's *he* doing here?"

The two of them tried to talk over each other. Trina fell silent and let Detective Deperro tell his story.

"Hey, honey," another man said. Then, "Who is *he*?"

Trina's sinuses burned, but damned if she'd let herself cry. "Boyd. You came."

He offered his charming smile. "Always."

She had the feeling he meant that literally.

Then she paid attention to what was happening out front. Two SUVs slammed to a stop, doors flying open as men jumped out. Four, five, six... eight. And Risvold, who must have scurried bent over as far as the rear of the sedan, straightened to meet his army.

"Eight men," she reported. "Nine, with Risvold. And...they're armed." Carrying what she was afraid were semiautomatic—or even fully automatic?—rifles that made the bolt-action Savage she'd been shooting seem useless. She focused on one of the men. "I think that's Ronald Pearson."

Gabe swiftly edged her aside and took a look. "In person," he murmured, before snapping out his next order. "Go unlock the gun cabinet."

She hustled. Once it was open, Gabe told her which of the remaining rifles he wanted.

Voice a little husky, he said, "Good, thanks," when she brought it to him.

Without asking, Boyd chose another for himself.

"You have something I can borrow?" the detective asked.

Boyd scrutinized him. "You any good with a rifle?"

"Trained as a sniper. Army," he added.

Boyd relaxed subtly. "All right, then."

Deperro hobbled over and took the last rifle. Watching Gabe's unrevealing back, Trina heard the bolt slide and knew Deperro was verifying that the weapon was loaded.

"Can somebody trade out the magazine for me?" she asked, hoping none of the men heard the tremor in her voice. "It should still have one cartridge loaded."

Boyd moved a lot like Gabe did, she suddenly realized. Both were almost uncannily graceful. Power was visible in their strides, but leashed. She doubted either ever broke so much as a twig underfoot.

"They're spreading out to surround us," Gabe said in a voice so level it raised the hair on the back of her neck. "Looks like a couple of them are carrying AK-47s, or something similar. Crap, there's either an AR-15 or an Omega 9mm. Boyd, did you call 911?"

"Yes. The sheriff's department doesn't have a great response time, but somebody should have been here." He muttered something under his breath. "I'd better call back. It wouldn't be good if a lone deputy rolled up right now."

"No."

He took his phone out.

"Just before I got here, I called a buddy with the DEA." It was Deperro speaking up. "Told him what I thought was happening."

"Did he take you seriously?" Gabe asked.

"Sounded like it. I wondered if they weren't already looking that direction."

"They likely to show up out here, or raid O.R.E.?"

"They'd damn well better show up," he growled.

Without so much as an acknowledging nod, Gabe said, "Trina, take Chloe upstairs. Tuck her in the bathtub. Ought to provide some protection. Then come down and take up a position behind the sofa. That'll make you central, and you'll be able to back any of us up."

She didn't argue. All three men were far more prepared for the ensuing battle than she could ever be.

Chloe's small body was stiff in her arms. She hurried upstairs, diverted to her bedroom to grab the comforter and the stuffed unicorn, then carried her into the bathroom. On her knees after settling the little girl in the tub, she stroked the soft red-gold hair. "I know this is scary, sweetie. But we'll be fine. I'll leave the door open so you can hear us. Okay?"

Chloe shivered harder, but her head did bob.

"Good. You're such a brave girl." Trina kissed her, then tore downstairs. The rifle and handgun lay behind the sofa, where Gabe wanted her.

Deperro knelt at the end of the short hall, where he could see into a room Gabe hadn't even furnished. A home office? In his fleeting visits, he wouldn't need anything like that.

Even in profile, she saw that the detective's skin tone was closer to gray than his usual bronze. The towel around his thigh was soaked. Blood dripped onto the polished plank floor.

"What's your first name?" she asked in a low voice.

He gave her a startled look. "Daniel."

A barrage of gunfire broke out, seemingly coming from all directions. Trina jerked as glass shattered. She could see only Deperro, who thrust the rifle around the doorframe and fired. Once, twice, again. She desperately wished she could see Gabe, but she heard him swearing as he fired.

Silence fell, interrupted by a phone ringing.

It was apparently Boyd's, because he said a few words she couldn't make out.

Then he raised his voice slightly. "Leon's set up in back."

"Anybody injured?" Gabe. "Should have said, any new injuries?"

The other two men both answered, "No."

"Trina?" he said sharply.

"I'm fine."

"Okay. My preference would be to hold them off without killing—not sure what my command structure would think about me taking out a bunch of drug traffickers while I'm rehabbing—but it's not looking like we're going to have any choice."

"My presence lends some legitimacy." Deperro's voice—Daniel's voice—came out thin.

Alarmed, Trina saw him close his eyes, wipe a forearm over his face.

"Let's trade places," she said, starting to crawl forward.

"No." He waved her back and resolutely squared his shoulders. "I'm good."

"You seeing any activity?" Boyd called.

"Zip." Gabe, sounding grim.

Barely seconds later, another burst of sound deafened Trina. Gunfire, and more. Deperro seemed to be yelling. An explosion powerful enough to shake the floor beneath Trina's knees sent the detective flying backward. He slammed into the wall, his rifle sliding along the floor toward Trina.

A second, equally powerful explosion came from the kitchen, a third from the front porch.

Terrified, Trina scrambled from the shelter of the sofa to flatten herself against the wall next to the hall. Gabe spared one look over his shoulder to see her, then resumed firing. She drew a deep breath for courage, leveled the rifle and spun to see the hall.

A bullet slammed into the wall inches from her chest. Her first shot took a man down, sending his handgun flying. He pushed himself to his knees and lunged forward for the gun. She shot again, hitting the floor in front and to one side of him.

"Flat on the floor!" she ordered. "Don't move or you're dead."

GABE HAD NEVER fought in a battle with his attention divided. But not once had he been able to quash his awareness of Trina. He hated knowing they needed her, that he couldn't tuck her away upstairs with Chloe. After hearing a bark that had to be her rifle, he called, "Trina?"

He was betting she'd never be fine again. But he'd been right; in the moment, she'd been willing to kill to ensure that those men wouldn't get their hands on Chloe.

Seeing no movement out front, Gabe risked turning. Trina stood with the barrel of the rifle alternately pointing at the man who lay flat on the floor and the open doorway beyond.

Thank God, Deperro stirred, shook his head. Blood dripped down one side of his face, but gradually he regained his wits. Showing his teeth, he torturously got to his knees, crawled forward and planted a knee in the middle of the guy's back. From a pocket, he produced plastic cuffs.

As he wrenched one hand behind the man's back, then the other, the guy glared at Trina, his face twisted in hate. Just for that look, Gabe wanted to shoot him. The son of a bitch didn't know how lucky he was that Gabe still held on to a modicum of self-control. Or was that sanity?

He had an almost amused thought. So much for those overanxious therapists back at the hospital. He'd gotten through surreal circumstances all but guaranteed to trigger flashbacks.

It's not over yet.

He turned his head and scanned the front. Because he'd pinned them there, he knew at least two men were crouched behind the row of SUVs, probably more. Pearson, for sure. He didn't seem to have joined the battle. Did he really think he could stay safe while everyone else took the risks? Too bad one of the traffickers hadn't gotten irritated and popped him.

Given what appeared to be another lull, Gabe raised his voice. "How many down?"

"I've got one who looks dead," Boyd reported.

"There's another guy out by the barn. One of Leon's, shots, I think. He's alive, but the way he's writhing, I'm guessing he took a bullet in his knee."

"I shot one." Trina sounded almost numb. "Daniel's hurt worse, but he handcuffed the guy."

"Deperro, did you take another bullet?"

"Just stunned," Deperro said coolly. "Grenade."

"Yeah, those were no flash-bangs," Gabe agreed. "I have a couple down, too. That leaves only four. I'm thinking they may run for it."

"Won't do Pearson any good to run," Boyd commented.

"Or Risvold." Deperro sounded utterly cold. Betrayal did that to a man.

They all heard an engine start. Gabe swore. "Looks like they don't mind leaving their buddies behind."

"Wouldn't it be good if…if they do leave?" For the first time, Trina's voice trembled.

About ready to expose himself to shoot some tires, Gabe cocked his head. "Sirens."

"Helicopter, coming fast," Boyd called from the back.

"Good guys or bad guys?"

"It's white with…can't see the insignia."

Good guys. Not that Gabe allowed himself to lose focus or let relief shut down the adrenaline, not yet. He'd seen men killed when they dropped their guard prematurely.

Flashing lights appearing through the trees. Two,

three…four law enforcement vehicles. Doors open, men taking position behind them with rifles pointed.

A voice boomed through a bullhorn. "Drop your weapons. Stand up slowly, hands in the air."

A second voice blasted from somewhere behind the cabin, too.

What looked like SWAT officers raced forward, yanked one man after another from behind the line of vehicles. Planted their faces against the side of the black SUVs, hands on the roof. With pleasure, Gabe watched Detective Risvold, Ronald Pearson and two other men being frisked.

At last, he lowered the Remington, leaned it against the wall and said in a rough voice, "Trina? Come here."

She flew to him. He yanked her too hard against him, afraid he was hurting her but realizing that for the first time in his damn life he was shaking and couldn't help himself. Yet she held him just as hard, and maybe it wasn't him who was shaking after all.

Finally, he touched his forehead to hers. "I've never been so scared before," he murmured. It was a minute before he could make himself release her and open the front door.

GABE DISLIKED DEALING with the aftermath as much as he had defending his cabin as if it were a plot of ground in Afghanistan. He sent Trina upstairs to take care of Chloe, and walked out beside the wheeled gurney carrying Deperro.

Just before he was lifted into the first ambulance, Gabe held out a hand. "Thank you, Detective. We might not have made it without you."

Deperro shook, offering a wan smile. "Daniel."

Gabe didn't trust easily, but this cop had proved himself. "Daniel," he said with a nod. "We'll be talking."

He waited until the ambulance doors closed before he looked around in astonishment. The four uninjured men, including Pearson and Risvold, had been hauled away immediately, behind the cage in two police cars. Gabe had watched as Pearson, face florid, had argued furiously as he was cuffed. Risvold hadn't said a word, blanched by shock until he looked like the walking dead.

The two men Gabe shot were being evaluated and treated here in front, along with the one Deperro had cuffed inside. Medics had trotted around back to look at the others. All waited their turns in other ambulances as they arrived.

Two DEA agents in body armor and the SWAT lieutenant closed in on him. "I'm told you're Gabe Decker," one of the agents said.

Boyd crossed the porch and came to join him. When one of the DEA guys looked askance at him, Gabe said shortly, "We co-own the ranch."

Boyd glanced over his shoulder. "Looks like they did a number on your cabin."

They all swept appraising looks at the front of the building. The porch railing and some of the boards were shredded. Jagged bits of glass clung in window frames. The door was badly scarred, as were sections of the log walls.

"Bullets would have ripped right through the walls if they hadn't been so solid," one of the men commented.

Gabe grunted. That wasn't why he'd built out of logs, but being bulletproof had certainly turned out to be a secondary benefit. "The grenade blasts inside did a lot of damage, too. Especially to the kitchen." But miraculously, none of them besides the detective had been injured. That's what mattered.

Trina and Chloe were safe. He had a feeling Trina could have held off the whole damn attack force alone if she'd had to. His heart beat out of rhythm as he pictured her at the top of the stairs, spraying bullets.

"We need you to tell us what happened, step by step," the same DEA agent said. They'd introduced themselves earlier, but it took Gabe a minute to summon his name.

Philip Zepeda, that was it. And the taller, older agent was Todd Carter.

"Anybody killed?" Gabe asked first.

"I'm told one of the two out back is in critical condition," the SWAT lieutenant said. "We have a Life Flight coming for him. Otherwise, they'll all recover to stand trial."

"Okay." Gabe suddenly realized both his thigh and one hip ached fiercely. To hell with pride. "You mind if we sit?" he asked. Without waiting for an answer, he walked over to take a seat on a porch step.

The older DEA guy joined him.

"Don't know if Detective Deperro had a chance to talk to you."

Zepeda's mouth tightened, but he finally nodded. "Briefly."

Boyd and Gabe told the story in turns, starting with the original murders and progressing through the leak that led to the arson fire and Trina's decision to go into hiding with Chloe. Gabe didn't offer details as to how he'd evaded notice when he drove Trina to and from work, but he did describe the attack on the highway as well as the black helicopter buzzing the ranch buildings. He talked until he was hoarse: Chloe finally telling them what she'd seen, his own trip to call Detective Deperro, what Deperro had said about why he'd followed his own partner out to the ranch and the confrontation that had left him with a bullet in his thigh.

Boyd put in his bits here and there. They'd considered leaving Leon out of this, but the bullets would be matched to weapons, so it was better to be honest.

When he finished, the SWAT lieutenant ran a hand over his close-shaved head. "Hell of a thing."

Boyd gave the DEA agents a hard stare. "I assume you didn't give the traffickers a chance to clean house at Open Range Electronics."

They exchanged a glance. Zepeda was apparently elected to be the mouthpiece, because he said, "The

possibility that the company played any part in drug
trafficking is still speculation." He cleared his throat.
"However, we had a warrant in hand, and acted on it
immediately after Detective Deperro's call. He and I
have worked on drug enforcement task forces together
in the past, so I placed a high reliance on his word."

His phone rang, and when he stepped away, the
gathering broke up. Gabe knew these had been only
the first of multiple interviews. It might be an eon
before his weapons were returned to him. Every one
that had been fired had been gathered as evidence. He
was indifferent to that; he hadn't so much as opened
the gun safe until Joseph's call asking him to keep
his sister safe.

Gabe hoped Trina was with him when the time
came to tell brother Joseph the whole story.

BY BEDTIME, GABE had hardly spoken to Trina since
he and she had packed up everything they'd need
for a day or two and taken Chloe to Boyd's larger
ranch house. Boyd had labored without a lot of help to
maintain some conversation at the dinner table. Gabe
spoke up only when asked a direct question. Trina
would have been furious with him if not for his tenderness toward Chloe, who'd burrowed in his arms
as often as she had in Trina's. Boyd's cook had had
the sense to serve a child-friendly meal, and while
Chloe had picked at her food, she *had* eaten.

It had taken longer to get her to sleep than usual,
too. Trina went back downstairs to join the men but

quickly wondered why she'd bothered. She was in that unpleasant state of being wired still and exhausted, too. Chatting with Boyd while Gabe watched her broodingly wasn't what she needed.

Suddenly having had enough, she jumped to her feet. "I think I'm ready for bed. I'll see you both in the morning."

Gabe rose, too. "I'll do the same."

As stirred up as she was, she almost wished he'd stayed downstairs. Once upstairs, she turned into the bathroom and shut the door practically in his face. Only, her skin prickled as she showered and brushed her teeth. Aroused, mad, hopeful, she opened the door. If he'd gone on to bed…

He was waiting. Any indignation she'd felt was washed away instantly at the expression on his face. He started kissing her before she had a chance to take a breath. Her desperation rose to meet his, and they barely reached his room before they made love with frantic, silent need. The second time was no less urgent.

In the wake of the astonishing pleasure, she concentrated on his heartbeat, on the warm chest beneath her hand. She had to keep her mouth shut. She had to. Whatever she wanted to believe, she really didn't know how he felt about her.

And, oh, she hated knowing that trying to push him would be the absolute wrong thing to do.

Once certain he was asleep, Trina slipped out of his bed and between cold sheets to join Chloe. She needed to be here when Chloe woke up. She hadn't the slightest doubt that the police would insist on hearing Chloe's testimony themselves, and soon. As in, tomorrow.

Morning found Chloe still frightened but, thank heavens, not mute. Accordingly, at midmorning a detective and the detective division lieutenant arrived to speak to her. Trina was permitted to sit on the sofa, but an arm's length from the little girl. She did understand that they needed to be certain she wasn't sending signals with her touch. Gabe had taken up a stance right behind the sofa, probably ready to glower if anyone dared upset Chloe.

Trina would have been a lot more apprehensive if this detective wasn't the woman she'd worked with before. This time, there were no snapped questions, no veiled impatience. Detective Melinda McIntosh got Chloe chattering about Mack and the foals here on the ranch, until she was relaxed and animated.

When the important question came, she said clearly, "I saw Uncle Ronald. I heard him and Daddy yelling before. Then there was a bang and Daddy fell down. And…and some more bangs. Uncle Ronald leaned over Daddy, only he didn't help Daddy up."

Only a few questions later, it was over. Boyd ushered the cops out while Gabe told Chloe the housekeeper had made something yummy just for her.

Trina stayed where she was, almost numb. There was no more reason to be afraid. She had her life back. She could rebuild her town house, or buy a different place. Go back to work. Talk to Chloe's grandmother.

So why didn't she even want to stand up?

She was staring blankly at the view through the enormous front window when Gabe walked in front of her. Then, of course, she couldn't see anything but him. Her gaze slowly lifted.

"Can we talk?" he asked.

He'd never said when his physical would take place. Had he put it off because of his promise to her brother?

"Oh, sure. If you'd like to sit down…"

"No, I don't want to be interrupted. Do you mind going for a walk?"

She nodded, rose to her feet as if she'd been preparing to bounce up any minute and verified that the housekeeper would keep an eye on Chloe.

Gabe didn't touch her, but outside he nodded toward a small stretch of wooded land, beyond which was a white-board fence enclosing a pasture. A small herd of horses grazed a distance away.

"What are you thinking you'll do now?" Gabe asked, after a couple of minutes of silence.

"Oh— Get new ID. Decide whether I want to rebuild or find someplace else to live. You know. Everything I had to put off." Striving to sound bright, she asked, "You?"

"I don't have any choice but to take my physical," Gabe said slowly. "I have another ten months on this enlistment."

Her heart sank.

They had reached the fence. Instead of leaning on it, he stopped and took her hands. "I don't want to leave you."

"I'm...not sure what that means."

"You may not feel the same...you probably don't. I don't have the education you do, or—" His vivid blue eyes showed stunning vulnerability. "You're nothing I ever expected, but... Damn." He blew out a long breath. "I'm in love with you, Trina. If you'd wait for me... You could stay in the cabin, so you wouldn't need to get another place. Once it's fixed up, I meant." Now he was talking fast, persuasively. "And that's only if I pass the physical."

The awful tightness in her chest had released as suddenly as a stretched rubber band, leaving her wobbly on her feet like a one-day-old foal.

She could ask him what he envisioned for his future, but she'd realized something in the past twenty-four hours. The powerful need to protect, to serve, was part of what she loved about him. There was no way she'd ask him to give up being a Ranger.

"I love you, too," she said simply. "Only...there's something you should know."

He had started to draw her closer but stopped. "What's that?"

"Chloe's grandmother or another relative may want her now, but I'm going to ask if they'd let me adopt her. I'd do everything I could to allow them to maintain a relationship with her, but... I love her."

Gabe groaned and pulled her into his arms. "I assumed we'd try to keep her. Don't keep scaring me."

"Having a child means—"

"I want you to marry me." Every word came out gritty. "Soon. So I'll know you're here, waiting for me."

Her vision blurred. "We could come with you, you know."

"I don't think I'll pass the physical," he told her. "If I do, I'll finish my enlistment, but then I'm done. The time was coming anyway. I'm ready to be a rancher."

"You're not saying this because you think it's what I want?"

Gabe shook his head. "No," he said quietly, bending to brush his mouth softly over hers. "I want to breed and train horses, help Boyd build this into the most successful ranch in Oregon."

Her smile felt luminous. "How would you feel about breeding a kid or two?"

This laugh was new, joyous. His guard had come crashing down. "I might have to look into your bloodlines..."

"Try telling that to Joseph."

He grunted as if she'd hit him. "He'll be my brother-in-law."

"Yes, he will."

"Lucky I already liked him," he said, just before he kissed her. And kept right on kissing her.

* * * * *

An absolute melee had begun.

Jasmine helped up a young man, a white-faced rising star in a new television series. He tried to thank her.

"Get out, go—walk quickly," she said.

There were no more gunshots. But would they begin again?

She made her way to Josef Smirnoff, ducking beneath the notice of his distracted bodyguards. She knelt by him as people raced around her. "Josef?" she said, reaching for his shoulder, turning him over.

Blood covered his chest. Covered him. There was no hope for the man; he was already dead, his eyes open in shock. There was blood on her now, blood on the designer gown she'd been wearing, everywhere.

She looked up; Jorge had to be somewhere nearby.

That's when she knew she was about to be attacked herself.

There was a man coming after her, reaching for her.

She rolled quickly, avoiding him once. But as she prepared to fight back, she felt as if she had been taken down by a linebacker. She stared up into the eyes of the shaggy-haired newcomer. Bright blue eyes, startling against his face and dark hair. She felt his hands on her, felt the strength in his hold.

No. She was going to take him down.

She jack-knifed her body, letting him use his own weight against himself, causing him to crash into the floor.

He was obviously surprised; it took him a second—but only a second—to spin himself. He was back on his feet in a hunched position, ready to spring at her.

Where the hell was Jorge?

She feinted, as if she would dive down to the left, dove to the right instead, and caught the man with a hard chop to the abdomen that should have stolen his breath.

He didn't give; she was suddenly tackled again, down on the ground, feeling the full power of the man's strength atop her. She stared up into his eyes, blue eyes, glistening ice at the moment.

She realized the crowd was gone; she could hear the bustle at the doorway, hear the police as they poured in at the entrance.

But right there, at that moment Josef Smirnoff lay dead in an ungodly pool of blood—blood she wore—just feet away.

And there was this man.

And herself.

"Hey!" Thank God, Jorge had found her.

He dove down beside them, as if joining the fight.

But he didn't help Jasmine; he made no move against the man. He lay by Jasmine, as if he'd just been floored himself.

He whispered urgently, "Stop! FBI, meet MDPD. Jasmine, he's undercover. Jacob... Jasmine is a cop. My partner."

The man couldn't have looked more surprised. Then he made a play of socking Jorge, and Jorge lay still.

Jacob stood and dragged Jasmine to her feet. For a long moment he looked into her eyes, and then he wrenched her elbow behind her back.

"Play it out," he said, "nothing else to do."

"Sure," Jasmine told him.

And as he led her out—toward Victor Kozak, who now stood in the front, ready to take charge, Jasmine managed to twist and deliver a hard right to his jaw.

He swirled her around again, staring at her, and rubbing his jaw with his free hand.

"Play it out," she said softly.

Don't miss
Undercover Connection
by New York Times *bestselling author Heather Graham,
available November 20, 2018, wherever
Harlequin® Intrigue books and ebooks are sold.*

www.Harlequin.com

Here's a sneak peek at Wrangler's Rescue
by New York Times *bestselling author B.J. Daniels.*

Ashley Jo "AJ" Somerfield couldn't help herself. She kept looking out the window of the Stagecoach Saloon hoping to see a familiar ranch pickup. Cyrus Cahill had promised to stop by as soon as he returned to Gilt Edge. He'd been gone for over a week now after going down to Denver to see about buying a bull for the ranch.

"I'll be back on Saturday," he'd said when he left. "Isn't that the day Billie Dee makes chicken and dumplings?"

He knew darned well it was. "*Texas* chicken and dumplings," AJ had corrected him since everything Billie Dee cooked had a little of her Southern spice in it. "I know you can't resist her cookin', so I guess I'll see you then."

He'd laughed. Oh, how she loved that laugh. "Maybe you will if you just happen to be tending bar on Saturday."

"I will be." That was something else he knew darned well.

He'd let out a whistle. "Then I guess I'll see you then."

She smiled to herself at the memory. It had taken Cyrus a while to come out of his shell. One of those "aw shucks, ma'am" kind of cowboys, he was so darned shy she thought she was going to have to throw herself on the floor at his boots for him to notice her. But once he had opened up a little, they'd started talking, joking around, getting to know each other.

Before he went out of town, they'd gone for a horseback ride through the autumn fallen leaves of the foothills up into the towering pines of the forest. It had been Cyrus's idea. They'd ridden up into one of the four mountain ranges that surrounded the town of Gilt Edge—and the Cahill Ranch.

It was when they'd stopped to admire the view from the mountaintop that overlooked the small western town that AJ had hoped Cyrus would kiss her. He sure looked as if he'd wanted to as they'd walked their horses to the edge of the overlook.

The sun warming them while the breeze whispered through the boughs of the nearby pine trees, it was one of those priceless Montana fall days before the weather turned and winter blew in. That was why Cyrus had said they should take advantage of the beautiful day before he left for Denver.

Standing on the edge of the mountain, he'd reached over and taken her hand in his. "Beautiful," he'd said. For a moment she thought he was talking about the view, but when she met his gaze she'd seen that he meant her.

Her heart had begun to pound. This was it. This was what she'd been hoping for. He drew her closer. Pushing back his Stetson, he bent toward her. His mouth was just a breath away from hers—when his mare nudged him with her nose.

She could laugh about it now. But if she hadn't grabbed Cyrus, he would have fallen down the mountainside.

"She's just jealous," Cyrus had said of his horse as he'd rubbed the beast's neck after getting his footing under himself again.

But the moment had been lost. They'd saddled up and ridden back to Cahill Ranch.

AJ still wanted that kiss more than anything. Maybe today when Cyrus returned home. After all, it had been his idea to stop by the saloon his brother and sister owned when he got back. She thought it wasn't just Billie Dee's chicken and dumplings he was after and bit her lower lip in anticipation.

Find out if AJ gets that kiss in the exciting conclusion of
The Montana Cahills series, available wherever
HQN Books are sold November 2018.

www.Harlequin.com